TRINITY

THE
HIDDEN
ENEMY

ZACK SATRIANI

Hodder
Children's
Books

A division of Hachette Children's Books

Produced by Hothouse Fiction – www.hothousefiction.com

First published in Great Britain in 2012
by Hodder Children's Books

1

A Catalogue record for this book is available from the British Library

ISBN 978 1 444 90660 8

Typeset in AGaramond Book by Avon DataSet Ltd,
Bidford on Avon, Warwickshire

Printed and bound by
CPI Group (UK) Ltd, Croydon, CR0 4YY

The paper and board used in this paperback by Hodder Children's Books
are natural recyclable products made from wood grown in
sustainable forests. The manufacturing processes conform to the
environmental regulations of the country of origin.

Hodder Children's Books
a division of Hachette Children's Books
338 Euston Road, London NW1 3BH
An Hachette UK company
www.hachette.co.uk

Look out for:

TRINITY 2: THE ASSASSIN
TRINITY 3: THE INVASION

**The fight to save Trinity has
never been so dangerous . . .**

With special thanks to Tom Bradman

Prologue

The rock drifted silently through space.

It had travelled an unknowable distance through the emptiness of the universe. For billions of years it had journeyed, crossing the grand sweep of galaxies and the immense nothingness between them. Centuries had passed since the rock last felt the pull of gravity.

But now it was drawn to a small yellow star, surrounded by three planets.

The first of the three worlds shone like a blue pearl in the darkness of space. No land showed anywhere on the perfect globe, just an endless expanse of water. A pair of titanic sea creatures, large enough to be seen from thousands of paces, gently broke the surface of the ocean-world before returning to the depths. As the rock passed, a billion living minds, all joined as one, reached out from the ocean in joyous greeting.

The rock moved on, silent.

Next it passed a large, craggy planet, pitted and

scarred by a thousand ancient volcanoes. But, though the landscape seemed lifeless, there were still signs of civilization. High-powered targeting lasers from a dozen weapon systems locked on the rock, alert for any danger. But there was no evidence of a threat, so the planet's guns remained still.

The rock continued on, as gravity tugged on its massive bulk.

It curved round the third planet. Life swarmed in a patchwork of forests and fields. On the night-side, the lights of great cities shone like a galaxy of stars. Around the planet spun hundreds of artificial moons – satellites that swept the rock with scanners, calculating its worth.

The rock moved past the verdant planet, then began its orbit around the star once more.

And deep beneath the surface, something stirred.

1

'It's not a bad deal you've put together there, lad,' said Tyrus, leaning back in his seat and scratching his thick, grey beard. 'I never thought I'd say this, but all right – I'll lease you the ships.'

Keller eyed him steadily. 'You won't regret it, Tyrus. Your share of the profits should be a tidy sum, once it's all up and running. I just need your print on the contract . . .'

He pushed the data-slate across the dark oak table to the older man, and held his breath. Every eye in the vaulted chamber was on him, from the life-size portraits of long-dead traders staring down from the walls, to the scrum of assistants, advisors and hangers-on standing either side of the long table, tracking the deal. Even though he couldn't see him, Keller knew his father was there too, watching. He recognized the particular hush that fell over a room whenever Cantor's trade king was present.

Tyrus picked up the slate and scanned through it one last time.

Come on, you avaricious old crow, thought Keller, his heart pounding. *Make the deal . . .*

The old man looked up into the teenager's eyes, as if to weigh his value. Then, without breaking eye contact, he pressed his thumb firmly on the contract. A cheer went up around the room as Tyrus passed the data-slate back to Keller.

'But I'm afraid your terms were far too generous, My Prince,' he said, a patronizing smile on his wrinkled face. 'You should have looked more closely at the space-harbour charges. They're all coming out of your share.'

Keller chuckled. 'Is that so, Tyrus? Then you're right, I should have looked more closely.' His shoulders shook, as the chuckle turned into a belly laugh.

The older man's eyes narrowed. 'I'm glad you think losing four thousand credits per turn is so amusing.'

'Oh, I'm not laughing about that,' replied Keller, wiping his streaming eyes.

'Then what *are* you laughing about?' Tyrus folded his arms, as he waited to hear the joke.

'You were so busy trying to fleece me on the space-harbour charges that you weren't paying attention to the maintenance estimates,' said Keller, grinning.

'They leave you paying all the costs while I take all the profits!'

'You *cheated* me?' roared Tyrus, standing so quickly his antique chair flew backwards. 'I'll have you in the Commerce Courts faster than you can say "breach of contract"!'

'Sit down, sit down,' said Keller, waving his hand. 'I haven't sealed the contract. It was never meant to be a real deal anyway. Why would I want ten of your rickety old space-hulks? Everyone knows they can hardly make it out of the system without breaking down. No, I just bet my friends that I could hire half of your fleet – and that you'd pay me for it too!'

As he spoke, Keller's friends crowded round, all trying to slap him on the back.

'Why you cocky little—' Tyrus stopped in mid-flow as a tall figure stepped out of the throng. Biting his lip, the old trader bowed. 'Your Majesty.'

'Don't worry, my friend,' said Trade King Lial, his deep voice carrying across the room. 'I will speak to my son about the importance of respect in negotiations. Keller, walk with me a moment.'

'Of course, Sire,' said Keller, following his father out of the palace's trade chamber and through an archway.

They walked slowly along a balcony overlooking the

palace gardens. Keller let his gaze wander across the landscape. Plants from all reaches of the galaxy flourished in the rich soil, and the sweet, spicy scent of flowering Circian orchids filled the air. To their left, alcoves in the wall held sculptures and statues from dozens of different worlds.

The gardens are a paradise, thought Keller. And well they should be – they'd cost enough.

'I don't understand why you waste your talents with such games.' King Lial sighed. 'If you made deals like that for real, you'd be a wealthy man in your own right by now.'

'What do I need money for?' Keller laughed. 'I'm a prince, and one day I'll be King of Cantor!'

'*Trade* King,' Lial snapped, a note of irritation entering his voice. 'A working king, a respected merchant who protects Cantorian interests in the intergalactic community! Believe me, you'll need men like Tyrus by your side then.'

Lial turned to his son and Keller looked back into his face. There could never be any doubt that they were father and son. The young prince had the same strong jaw and sharp nose as his father, but where Keller's hair was jet black, Lial's was now pure white. The older man's skin seemed dry and thin, and creases and wrinkles spread out from his eyes and the sides of his mouth when he talked.

How old is he now? Keller wondered. *Eighty turns? Ninety?*

'It was a good trick, father,' said Keller, risking a smile.

'That it was,' said Lial, an identical grin spreading across his face. 'The look on that old skinflint's face . . .' He slapped his son on the shoulder and the pair started walking again. 'But we have something serious to talk about. This morning I received a com from General Iccus.'

Keller curled his lip. 'The Bellori leader?'

Lial nodded. 'It's about the asteroid.'

'Surely they must have seen sense by now?'

'Quite the contrary. The Bellori are refusing to consider any mining activity.'

'The mullocks,' growled Keller. 'Don't they realize the value of the detrillium in that rock?'

'Their priorities are different to ours. They want to use it as a military base.'

Keller ground his teeth in frustration. 'Can't they see that if we mine it, we'll *all* get rich and then they can buy as many warships as they like?'

'It seems not.' King Lial shrugged. 'Anyway, the

7

Bellori aren't our only problem. The Aquanths are claiming that the asteroid is sacred.'

Keller's eyes bulged. 'You *are* joking?'

'I wish I was.'

'But that's . . . that's . . . that's just the craziest thing I've ever heard,' spluttered Keller. 'How can a floating lump of space-rock be *holy*?'

'Lady Moa says that it is the "Heavenly Messenger" mentioned in their prophecies. Apparently, its arrival marks a new era of cooperation and harmony between our three planets.'

Keller shook his head. 'That high priestess has been living under the sea for too long. *A new era of cooperation and harmony . . .*'

'Well there's no sign of it so far,' said King Lial. 'None of us seem willing to budge.'

'So what happens now?'

'I've suggested a meeting – a conference of the three leaders to discuss how to proceed.'

'When are they coming?' Keller asked, making a mental note to be away at the time. It would be just his luck to get caught up in all the tedious politics.

'That's the problem,' replied the trade king with a grimace. 'They aren't.'

'What do you mean?'

'Iccus won't agree to meet anywhere other than on the asteroid itself. It's the only place the Bellori consider neutral ground.'

'Mullocks,' muttered Keller again.

'Perhaps,' said his father. 'But we can't risk offending them, or trade in the Trinity System will be affected, and then we all pay.'

Keller frowned. 'Why are you telling me all this anyway?'

'Because you'll be joining me as part of the Cantorian delegation.'

'What?' Keller's face fell. 'But the Kaloon Derby is in three cycles,' he protested. He could already picture the after-party . . .

'This is state business,' Lial said firmly, clapping a strong hand down on his son's shoulder. 'And that comes before pleasure. It's time for you to learn about real negotiations . . .'

2

Dray hefted her *cthunga* sword in both hands and glared at the enemy before her.

It was like staring into a mirror. Two and a half paces tall, every inch of her opponent's body was covered with overlapping grey plates, ridged like the hide of a lava crocodile, capable of deflecting all but the sharpest blades and even some projected-energy weapons; eye-slits and mouth-opening too small to get an arrow into. Bellori armoured skin – *Brilliant when you are under attack*, Dray thought, glancing down at her own keratin plates, *but not so good when you're the one doing the attacking* . . .

Keeping her sword raised, Dray warily circled the other fighter, looking for an advantage, assessing the ways she could bring him down. Garal was strong and he was fast, but he had to have a weakness . . .

Dray's com-link flashed. As her eyes flicked sideways to look at it, her opponent struck, his heavy blade slamming into her shoulder plate. The blow wasn't strong enough to break through, but the surprise knocked her off balance. Cursing herself for being so easily distracted, Dray swerved just as Garal swung a club-like fist at her face. She leaned backwards, bringing her left arm up to block the blow and swinging her sword low with her right. Her blade blurred through the air, only to be parried neatly by her rival's axe-shaft in a shower of sparks.

With a yell, Dray brought her weapon back up in an overhead chop. Garal went to block, but at the last moment she reversed her grip and brought the sword's pommel slamming down on to the axe-blade, shattering it. A powerful kick to the chest sent the larger warrior tumbling backwards. He hit the deck hard. In a click, Dray was on top of him, pressing her blade to the hairline join between the plates at the base of his neck. Dray smiled with satisfaction. One push and his head would be severed.

'Very impressive,' said a harsh voice. 'You fight almost like a warrior. A shame you'll never know the thrill of *real* combat.'

Dray looked up to see the bulk of another male filling the doorway, his red eyes shining with amusement. It was Sudor, captain of the special forces unit.

'These are my private training quarters, Sudor,' she said, feeling her grip on the sword tighten instinctively. 'You better have a good reason for this interruption, or you'll learn just how well I fight – first hand.'

Sudor flexed his thick neck, the keratin armour grinding together. 'While I'm sure you would be a formidable challenge, my dear,' he said in a voice slick with sarcasm, 'your father would never forgive me if you came to any harm.'

Dray bridled. Sudor always knew how to get right under her plates. She was a Bellori warrior. She didn't need anyone to protect her, or give her an easy ride.

'What do you want, Sudor?'

'The commander-in-chief sent me to find you – since you weren't answering his coms.'

Dray groaned inwardly. It had to have been her father calling. Reaching down, she helped Garal to his feet. The two Bellori bowed to each other before she turned to face Sudor.

'Have we arrived?'

Sudor nodded his massive head. 'We are starting our final approach now. The asteroid has settled into a stable orbit at the edge of the Trinity star's gravitational field. The position is perfect – even a *civilian* like you should be able to appreciate it. With a military outpost here we will make the Trinity System impenetrable.'

Dray forced herself to ignore Sudor's jibe. 'Even if we can persuade the Cantorians, the Aquanths will never agree.'

Sudor ground his fist against the doorway, leaving a dent in the metal. 'They will have no choice. The fish-folk are weak, and as for those Cantorian shopkeepers, pah! They would sell their own firstborn son for a handful of beans.'

Dray snorted. 'You're a fool, Sudor – simplistic to the point of stupidity. The Cantorians may have no honour, but they are devious negotiators. If they think the asteroid is worth something to them, it won't be easy to persuade them to give up their claim.'

Sudor stiffened. 'You insult me. If you were any more than a child, I'd—'

'What? Challenge me to a duel?' Dray's eyes flashed. 'Go ahead.'

For a moment, Dray thought the big male might actually do it. But then she saw his body relax.

'Your father is waiting. You may find he is a devious negotiator too.'

Intrigued, Dray stomped out through the door and followed Sudor along the narrow corridor to the cramped control deck. As she reached the mountainous figure sitting in the control chair, she came smartly to attention and raised her fist proudly overhead in the traditional Bellori salute.

Almost half as big again as the largest of his subordinates, General Iccus carried the scars of hundreds of combats. As a young warrior, the Bellori commander-in-chief had been a hero of the Vuzok Wars, defending the Trinity System from invasion. Since the Vuzoks' defeat, no battles had been fought within the Trinity System, but General Iccus and his troops had been deployed on many peacekeeping missions in distant galaxies.

Bulky crewmen sat at terminals around General Iccus, maintaining the *Astyanax*, the Bellori flagship, in perfect battle readiness. The view-screen showed the asteroid straight ahead, the makeshift convention centre a tiny gleam on the surface of the dark rock.

'Dray.' The general's low voice seemed to roll out across the room. 'Why didn't you answer my com?'

'I'm sorry, sir,' replied Dray. 'I was sparring with Garal.'

'Did you win?'

Dray pulled herself up proudly. 'Yes, sir.'

Iccus grunted. 'He's probably still suffering from that leg injury.'

'Very likely, sir,' agreed Sudor.

Dray felt her blood burn. 'He was perfectly fit,' she snapped.

Iccus turned his giant head to look at his daughter for the first time.

'He was perfectly fit, *sir*,' she corrected herself.

'Well . . . A victory is a victory, I suppose,' he rumbled. 'Although there is little honour in defeating a wounded opponent. Anyway, I have decided that you will join my personal bodyguard for these "negotiations".'

Dray felt her heart leap. At last – a proper assignment! Even if it wasn't a combat mission, it was a chance to prove herself. She shot a triumphant glance at Sudor.

'Thank you, sir. I am honoured.'

'There should be little danger,' said Iccus. 'But there may be other . . . opportunities. The Cantorian and the Aquanth heirs will also be present at the conference. Both males; both about your age.'

Dray's excitement vaporized. How could she have been foolish enough to think that her father might have chosen her for her fighting prowess? She was a bargaining chip, nothing more.

Every Bellori cadet was taught tactics and strategy, and Dray understood that a strategic marriage between ruling families was a potentially invaluable tool. It was all very well in theory, but it felt different when it was *her* life that was being decided. Not that it mattered. She was Bellori; she would do her duty.

'Of course, sir,' she replied, bunching her fists until her armour almost cracked. She could feel Sudor's glee as her father gestured him forward to talk about final preparations, and had to fight a rising wave of anger and frustration. Her father hadn't even bothered to dismiss her. He would never treat her like this if she was a *male*. Dray stared at the two hulking warriors hunched over the command panel, side by side. Like father and son. *Her* father and the son he wished he'd had.

Turning on her heel, Dray made for the door.

'Sir,' one of the officers interrupted, 'I've detected a Cantorian vessel on an approach vector to the asteroid. They're attempting to move ahead of us.'

'Those kracking farmers,' cursed Iccus. 'Increase thrust!'

The deck beneath Dray's feet started to vibrate and she grabbed hold of a terminal to keep her balance.

'They're matching our acceleration, sir,' called the officer.

'Engage weapons,' Sudor growled.

'No,' General Iccus commanded. 'This is not a battle. But we are the Bellori – we will not be beaten by *merchants*!' He spat the last word in disgust. 'More thrust!'

3

As the spaceship prepared to land, the water in the passenger tank sloshed and Ayl's stomach churned. It was an honour to be travelling to the Heavenly Messenger with his mother, the high priestess, but Ayl couldn't help wishing he were halfway across the Trinity System. If he couldn't be back home in Aquanthis in body, at least he could be there in his mind.

Ayl let his thoughts carry him to his home planet where soft light diffracted through the water, throwing faint patterns over his blue skin. His gills opened and shut gently as he gazed at the sight before him. The ocean was crowded with a mass of bodies. Thousands of Aquanths had gathered on the colourful reef before the Great Temple, countless silver fish darting around their long, graceful limbs. Above them the brilliant blue waters echoed with the music of a pair of gigantic chi-whales, their song filling the ocean with melody like a hymn to life itself.

Ever since the Heavenly Messenger had been seen in the skies above Aquanthis, its people had been filled with joy. In his mind, Ayl could feel the excitement and anticipation of the crowd mounting with every passing click. But he didn't share it. All he could feel was worry.

As if sensing his fear, his mother, Lady Moa, appeared beside him and took his hand. Ayl felt his mind slipping free of Aquanthis and its people. Slowly, he drifted away from them, until their thoughts and emotions were nothing more than a tiny tingle at the back of his brain.

Calm yourself, my child. They are all wishing us luck.

Ayl's gills trembled nervously. *But there are so many, and they expect so much.*

You do not bear that burden alone, Ayl. We all share it.

But the Bellori and the Cantorians – Ayl's history lessons weighed heavily on him: the violence and aggression of General Iccus; the base greed of Trade King Lial – *how can we make them see the Heavenly Messenger for what it truly is?*

The high priestess smiled. *Their link to The Divine is weak. It is our task to guide them to the truth, though they might not know it.*

Can we not just show them?

That is not possible. You know that, Ayl.

Yes, mother.

Ayl closed his eyes, remembering the amazement he had felt when his tutor had told him that the Bellori and Cantorians could not share their minds as every Aquanth could. He couldn't imagine what it must be like to live entirely in one head, cut off from the emotions of everyone around you.

Still, he thought, *perhaps it might sometimes be pleasant to be able to keep my thoughts to myself.*

Ayl, admonished his mother gently. *You cannot change who you are. And one day you will realize that you would not want to, even if you could. There is such strength in unity. I hope you never discover the loneliness of being an individual. Come, we have arrived.*

Ayl stepped off the ship that had brought the Aquanths across the great ocean of space, on to the rocky surface of the Heavenly Messenger. His feet, designed to propel him swiftly through the water, felt tender on the rough terrain.

His people had been waiting for the prophecy to be fulfilled for more than a thousand turns. They were certain that the asteroid was the Heavenly Messenger foretold by the scriptures – a wonderful sacred coming that would bring new knowledge of The Divine. As the Aquanth delegates walked awkwardly to the conference centre, Ayl waited for a rush of spiritual awareness. But there was nothing. If this was such a holy place then why couldn't he feel anything?

He found it hard to believe that the others weren't disappointed as well, but then perhaps their faith was stronger. Ayl could feel only calm determination in the group's mind, and the belief that they would make the other planets recognize the Heavenly Messenger for what it really was. If only he shared their certainty.

Beside him, Ayl's mother smiled. *All will be revealed*, she thought.

As the Aquanths entered the main hall of the conference centre, Ayl looked around the large dome, which had been hastily constructed on the asteroid's surface for the negotiations. Holo-screens had been set up, cycling through images of the three planets of the Trinity System, and the walls had been hung with dozens of banners, but the whole effect was one of temporary luxury. Ayl shifted uncomfortably. The strain of using his lungs instead of his gills was tiring, and the hot lights were drying out his skin. He longed for the cool embrace of water. But it wasn't the heat or the air that were bothering him most – it was an overwhelming sense of disappointment.

A young priest looked up from his hand console.

My lady, the other leaders have landed. They are on their way.

'Excellent,' said the high priestess. 'Let us remember to speak openly before our brothers. I am sure we will soon resolve our differences in peace and friendship.'

As she spoke, the door at the far end of the main hall irised open and two men walked in. To Ayl's eyes, they couldn't have been more different. One, a white-haired man carrying a silver cane, was wearing an immaculate tailored suit of rich gold fabric. The other, who loomed over the first by at least a head, didn't appear to be wearing any clothes at all – his body was covered by scarred keratin plates. Both were shouting.

'You could have killed us all,' the Cantorian yelled. 'That lumbering hulk of yours should never have been going so fast!'

'Well, you *traders* need to show some respect for the warriors that keep you safe,' roared the Bellori commander-in-chief, looming over the old trade king. His hands were balled into tight fists, making them look like great metal maces.

Ayl turned to his mother, eyes wide. The high priestess gave her son a tight smile. There was certainly nothing sacred about the men's behaviour.

4

It had taken Keller less than ten minutes to realize that the negotiations were going to be a complete disaster.

Even the decision as to who was going to sit where during the grand banquet that opened the conference had required half an hour of intense debate. Keller still couldn't understand why General Iccus objected so strongly to being placed on the left-hand table, unless he was worried about being outflanked by the platoon of black-uniformed waiters. In the end, the Bellori declared that using chairs was a sign of weakness and that they wouldn't sit down at all. Instead they lined up against one wall, chewing on the military rations they had brought from their warship. Keller almost felt sorry for them. He was sure that nutritionally the colourless bars ticked all the right boxes, but they looked anything but exciting.

The same could not be said for the dishes from Aquanthis. If anything, they were too interesting. Keller couldn't help wrinkling his nose as he caught another whiff of the potent stink rising from the platters of raw seaweed and steamed sea-tubers that had been placed in front of the blue-skinned delegation. However, it didn't seem to bother the Aquanths, who were rocking back and forth in their seats, swaying their heads over the food as if they were in some sort of rapture. Keller sniffed dubiously. Maybe living underwater had dulled their sense of smell.

He was just glad the Cantorians had some *proper* food. A whole leg of quantook and plenty of gravy for the vegetables. Rich food, and filling too. He sank his teeth into another forkful of the succulent meat and sighed with pleasure.

'Maybe this trip won't be all bad,' he muttered, leaning across to his neighbour, a grizzled trader of forty-odd turns named Yall.

'I'm sure your father will secure the mineral rights for Cantor, Your Highness,' replied Yall seriously.

'Oh, I'm not talking about *that*,' burped Keller, waving his knife expansively. 'I meant the food. Though, if we're really lucky, the talks might finish early enough for us to get back before the racing season is over.'

Yall nodded, a half-smile plastered on his face.

'Not that this "mission" hasn't had its entertaining

moments,' Keller added, a grin spreading across his face. 'Watching my father facing off with General Iccus was pretty impressive. He needs to be careful, though. These Bellori are a bit like my Inui Hunting Hounds back home – they need to be shown who's boss every now and then, but if you go too far, you'll find yourself on the wrong end of a very sharp object, if you get my meaning.'

Yall's smile was more like a grimace now.

Casting his gaze lazily around the room, Keller locked eyes with a Bellori warrior. The soldier's immobile face gave nothing away, but his chest plates rose and stiffened. Keller glanced down the coat of arms branded on to the keratin shell. It looked almost – no, *exactly* – the same as the one on General Iccus's chest plate.

Keller frowned. His father was always telling him how knowing your opponent was the most important advantage in any negotiation, and during the space voyage to the asteroid, he had forced Keller to memorize a list of every single Aquanth priest and Bellori warrior attending the conference. He knew the names, the clans – even the eye colour – of every delegate in the hall.

So how could he have forgotten that General Iccus had a son?

* * *

Ayl looked nervously from face to face, anxiety welling up in his mind. He wished he understood what was happening, but the emotions flickering from the Bellori and Cantorian delegations were so confusing. Tight, controlled waves of aggression spread out from the warriors while the traders seemed calm. Beneath the surface though, Ayl could sense that King Lial's thoughts never stopped flowing.

The young Aquanth chewed his lip. How annoying it was that the minds of the Bellori and Cantorians were closed to him. It was so *inefficient*. How could they possibly understand what each other wanted when they were so isolated from even their own people?

As he pushed his tubers around the plate, he watched the dark-haired boy sitting next to the trade king. The Cantorian was chewing a mouthful of dead animal flesh with such relish it was unbelievable. Ayl shuddered. Perhaps he should be grateful their minds weren't open to him. If they were so far from The Divine that they couldn't understand how wrong it was to eat other living creatures, how were they ever going to appreciate the significance of the Heavenly Messenger?

His mother put a cool hand on top of his. *This is a good opportunity for you to learn about our unenlightened*

26

brothers and sisters. Make the most of it.

The high priestess pushed back her chair with a low grating sound and began to stand. One of the Bellori guards jumped forwards and for an instant Ayl was scared they might be attacked. But then he saw Iccus staring at the soldier. The smaller warrior seemed to shrink under the general's gaze as he took his place again.

'Fellow residents of the Trinity System,' Ayl's mother said, acting as though the Bellori hadn't almost caused a diplomatic incident. 'I believe the time has come to begin our discussions.'

General Iccus stepped forward. 'She's right. Let's get this over with, so we can get back to more important matters – like keeping the Trinity System safe.'

His immense bulk made Ayl feel tiny and weak, but the disdain that came through in the man's voice made him despair. They had to negotiate with this barbarian, and he sounded as though he saw the Aquanths and the Cantorians as lower races.

'Before we start,' he rumbled, 'we should set out some rules of engagement. This is a high-security meeting. We should only allow essential personnel into the conference chamber.' There was a low growl of agreement from the rest of the Bellori.

'What do you propose then?' asked Trade King Lial caustically. 'The children are a little old to be sent outside to play.' The men at his table laughed.

It was all so tiresome. Ayl just wished they could say what they meant for once and stop trying to score points. The Cantorians went quiet as Iccus raised his fist.

'Back on Bellus, we have a saying – warriors are not born, they are *trained*.' Iccus pounded his fist into the table, making the cutlery shake. 'And experience is the greatest teacher of all. Our children – the heirs to our empires – need experience.' The general nodded at each of his fellow leaders. 'After all, none of us is getting any younger.'

The high priestess furrowed her brow. 'What are you suggesting, General?'

'I propose that these three, the rulers of tomorrow, should hold parallel talks. Maybe they'll come up with a new approach to our dilemma.'

General Iccus was hiding something, that much was clear from the tone of his voice, but Ayl couldn't tell what – or why. There was something behind the Bellori's suggestion, though, he was sure.

Trade King Lial had picked up on it too. Ayl could sense the man's suspicion, spiked with frustration with his own lack of understanding. None of these emotions showed on the trade king's face, though, which was as impassive as a mask.

His mother, however, was smiling to show her agreement.

Please, no, thought Ayl.

You must, my son, Moa replied. *Perhaps you can find some common ground for us all.*

What can we possibly share with these aliens? he wondered.

Dray felt shame flood her body. A bodyguard's place was beside her leader, protecting him from harm. To be sent away was a terrible dishonour. And for what? To play at *politics* with two spineless boys . . .

Was this some kind of punishment? Was she being sent away because she had jumped when the high priestess had stood? She'd been so keyed up, so tense. She hadn't moved so much as a toe plate for most of the meal, even though she'd had an agonizing cramp in her left leg. She'd been looking at the Cantorians, not seeing the blue-skinned pacifists as any real threat, when she heard Lady Moa move her chair. Instinct had kicked in and the next thing she knew her father was glowering at her. She'd let herself down. Again.

'What an interesting idea,' said King Lial, smiling broadly from across the table. 'I second the proposal. This is my son, Trade Prince Keller.'

The teenager stood up slowly, still chewing his food and looking around the room like he owned it.

So that's the Trade Prince of Cantor, she thought. *What a flabby waste of air.* The way the rest of the merchants had shovelled down their food, it was a wonder they weren't all as fat as the boy. No discipline at all.

'And this,' boomed her father, waving a hand towards her, 'is my daughter, Dray.'

She began to step forward but stopped when the trade prince started coughing. 'A girl!' he choked, spitting out his food. Dray felt her blood boil.

'Keller!' hissed the trade king.

'Sorry,' said the boy, speaking to his father. 'But she's so big! I . . .' The trade prince went quiet as he looked around. Every delegate in the room was staring at him. He turned back to Dray. 'Sorry.'

She glared at him, clenching her fists. She was going to make him suffer for that one day. And suffer badly. After a moment of tense silence, the high priestess spoke.

'This is my son, Ayl. We are honoured he will meet

your heirs.' The Aquanth stood awkwardly, looking everywhere but at the other two teenagers.

An imbecile, a weakling and a warrior, thought Dray. *It's like a bad joke.*

'Well, I suppose we had better get on with it,' grunted her father.

King Lial nodded. 'The youngsters can remain here while we adjourn to the conference chamber.'

'Very well,' said the high priestess. 'This way, gentlemen.'

With a nod to her son, the Aquanths' leader led the way out of the room. King Lial followed, patting Keller on the back as he went. General Iccus was last. As he passed Dray, the huge Bellori leaned towards his daughter, placing one hand on her broad shoulder.

'I need you to get on well with these two,' he whispered. 'Do you understand?'

Realization hit her like a punch to the gut. Her father wasn't interested in parallel talks at all – his suggestion was nothing but a feint, an elaborate ruse to get her alone with the heirs of the other two planets.

Dray's blood boiled. Her father was following his own agenda as usual. But what choice did she have?

'Yes, sir,' she said, choking out the last word.

Her father nodded then turned and left. The

remaining delegates from all three planets quickly followed their leaders. Finally, the room was empty apart from the three young people.

Dray paced angrily up and down beside the door, as if she would rather be anywhere else. She'd even prefer to be back on the *Astyanax* with Sudor. The captain had been visibly annoyed when General Iccus ordered him to patrol the Trinity System during the conference, but now Dray could see that Sudor had got the better deal. At least he was *doing* something on the flagship, while she was stuck in a room *talking*. As if that ever solved anything.

Ayl stood awkwardly, shifting from foot to foot. Keller threw himself back into his chair and picked idly at a bone.

'So,' the Cantorian said. 'Here we are . . .'

He was lucky Dray hadn't killed him already.

5

Ayl wrung his hands uncomfortably as the trade prince continued talking.

'I suppose we could make you each a one-off payment in return for letting us mine,' Keller said, leaning back in his chair and putting his hands behind his head. 'Enough to buy a few more warships for Bellus and another temple for Aquanthis.'

Ayl flinched inwardly as Dray stared murderously at Keller.

'Your arrogance is incredible!' she snapped. 'This asteroid is in an orbit that can monitor every space-lane in the sector. It's vital that a military base is built here immediately to protect all of our worlds, Cantor included.'

'Protect us?' Keller gave a sarcastic laugh. 'From what? Bellus, Cantor and Aquanthis are the only inhabited planets in the Trinity System, and your beloved fleet is more than big enough to combat any threat from further away than that. Unless you don't have as much faith in Bellori warriors as I do . . .' He folded his arms over his chest smugly.

Dray snorted.

'What do you think, Ayl?' Keller continued smoothly.

Ayl jumped. He had been trying to link minds with his mother to find out what was going on in the real negotiations, and had been only half-aware that the others were still speaking.

'This place is holy to my people,' he said. 'We believe it will bring unity to our three races. It will teach you of The Divine.'

For a moment Keller just stared at him. 'OK,' he said finally. 'Then I hope The Divine pays well, because some of us need to make a living. This chunk of rock is worth a fortune – several hundred fortunes, in fact. More than enough for you people to be able to buy as much of The Divine, or as much security, as you want.'

'Mining would completely ruin any military value this asteroid has,' Dray shouted. 'Not everything is for sale, Cantorian!'

As if you could buy *The Divine*, Ayl thought. Was the trade prince really so ignorant? As for the Bellori, to think – even for a click – that the Heavenly Messenger should be defiled by weapons of war . . .

Turning away, Ayl tried to block out the continued bickering and focused on his mother. Nothing they said in here would make any difference anyway. The real power was in the conference chamber, wielded by their parents. Ayl's consciousness floated through the walls and rooms of the building until it found the familiar pattern of the high priestess's thoughts.

Ayl! Why are you not concentrating on your discussions?

I have tried, mother. All they do is argue.

You must be patient, Ayl. Their fathers are just the same. Look . . .

For a moment, Ayl's vision swam, and then he was watching and listening through Lady Moa's eyes and ears as General Iccus ranted on about the urgent need to transform the asteroid into a military base.

Remember that it is not their fault, Ayl. They don't have the wisdom to understand. It's up to us to make them see that—

Ayl flinched as his mother's words were interrupted by an ear-splitting screech. It was high and hideous – like the sound of metal grating against metal – and it grew louder and louder until Ayl thought he couldn't stand it. Then, as suddenly as it had started, it stopped.

35

Mother? What was that?

I don't know.

As the screech died away, it was replaced by a strange scratching, chittering sound. Still linked to his mother's mind, Ayl could hear exactly where it was coming from.

There's something outside, Mother.

Trade King Lial had turned to the door too, confusion written on his face. The scratching was growing louder with every passing click.

Ayl, my son. The high priestess's thoughts were filled with concern. *I must break minds with you for a moment.*

What? No! What's happening?

General Iccus was on his feet now, calling for his bodyguards. Then the scratching reached a crescendo and suddenly the door opened. For an instant, Ayl caught a glimpse of what lay beyond. Then, as if a blade had sliced through the link with his mother, his mind went blank.

'What the—'

Dray leaped forward as Ayl slumped to the floor.

'What did you do to him?' demanded Keller.

'I didn't do anything,' replied Dray irritably, crouching over the prone body. 'He just fainted.'

'Well, give him some room,' said Keller. 'I think he's coming around.'

As he spoke, Ayl's double-eyelids flickered open.

'Easy now,' Keller said, patting Ayl's shoulder in what he hoped was a reassuring way. 'Are you OK?'

Ayl gasped and his whole body convulsed.

'Mother!' he cried.

Keller rolled his eyes. Trust his luck to be stuck with a mummy's boy.

'Your mother is not here,' said Dray bluntly. 'Do you require medical assistance?'

'Help them!' Ayl shouted. 'Help them!'

Keller shook his head. 'Help who?'

'My head,' moaned Ayl. 'Hurts . . .'

Dray stepped back, thumbing her com-link. 'Medic? Come in, medic.' The big Bellori growled. 'It's no good. The system's crashed or something. I can't get a connection.'

'He doesn't need a doctor,' snapped Keller. 'Not one of *your* battlefield butchers anyway.'

'Bellori medics are the finest in the galaxy!'

'Yeah,' Keller shot back. 'If you want your headache treated with a lobotomy!'

Dray stepped towards him menacingly, but before she could say anything more, Ayl suddenly sat bolt upright.

'They're coming!' he screamed, his eyes wide with terror.

For the first time, Keller felt a flicker of unease.

'What do you mean?' he asked, but Ayl had already slumped back to the ground, muttering incoherently. Dray stood over them both, hands on hips.

'What is going on here?' she snapped. 'Who's coming?'

As if in answer, the harsh braying of an alarm began to sound. The light changed suddenly from plain white to flashing red.

Keller clamped his hands over his ears. 'Now what?'

Dray was pressing her com-link again. 'Come in, General. General? Father?'

'Ayl,' said Keller urgently. 'What's wrong?'

'*Alum na ve rah sooo*,' mumbled Ayl. '*Alum na ve rah sooo.*'

Keller ground his teeth in frustration. He could feel panic building like a tidal wave inside him. 'This is no time for praying!'

Taking two steps forward, Dray brushed Keller aside, seized Ayl by the front of his loose-fitting tunic, hauled him to his feet and shook him violently.

'What the krack is happening, fish-boy!' she bellowed.

Ayl's eyes flew open.

'There's something here,' he said. 'We're under attack.'

Dray took a deep breath, exhilaration filling her. At last, some action. A chance to show her father what she was capable of. Suddenly, she was back in her element.

'An attack?' she said briskly. 'How do you know?'

'I saw it,' Ayl mumbled, his head lolling from side to side as if he was trying to shake off the effects of a punch.

'What are you talking about? You haven't left the room.' Dray lifted Ayl right off his feet and shook him roughly.

'Stop it, you're hurting him,' cried Keller. 'Put him down.'

With a grunt, Dray dropped Ayl back to the floor. He stood, swaying for a moment, then slumped back to the ground, wrapping his thin arms around his body.

'We have to find the rest of the delegation,' Dray said, thumping a fist into the opposite palm. 'I won't leave the commander-in-chief unprotected.'

'He's not unprotected,' Keller fired back. 'He's got ten Bellori warriors with him. What difference are you going to make?'

Dray stared murderously at Keller. If her father hadn't given her a direct order to be nice to the Cantorian prince, she would have cheerfully ripped off his arm and used it to beat the smug look off his face.

'Fine. You hide in here like a coward if you want to,' she spat. 'I'm going to find my father.'

'Wait a minute,' Keller protested. 'What about us?'

Dray stared contemptuously at the trade prince's shocked expression. He clearly couldn't believe that for once he wasn't the centre of attention. The gutless brat had probably never had to fend for himself for more than ten minutes in his whole life.

'What *about* you?'

'Well, you can't just leave us,' Keller squawked. 'What if something happens?'

'Listen, Cantorian,' said Dray, lowering her voice for emphasis. 'I'm going to find my commanding officer. You can either come with me, or you can stay here and hope that whatever's attacking us doesn't find you before I get back.'

Keller licked his lips nervously. 'All right, we'll come.'

'Help him up,' said Dray, with a curt nod at Ayl, 'and follow me.' She was already halfway to the door.

Keller hauled Ayl to his feet. The Aquanth seemed to be in some kind of a trance, but he staggered along as Keller pulled him. Dray moved to one side of the entrance and stood with her broad back to the wall. There was no telling what might be outside, and only one way to find out. She palmed the control panel and the door swirled open smoothly. Leaning out cautiously, she checked the corridor. Nothing. Just the blare of the alarm and the flashing of the emergency lights. Dray swore under her breath. On Bellus, there would have been a platoon of warriors already charging towards the conference hall. All she had was a half-conscious fish-boy and one flabby Cantorian.

'Come on,' she hissed, beckoning them forwards. 'And be quiet.'

Silently, she slipped out into the corridor, turning right. But after only a few paces, she froze. Something wasn't right.

Struggling to hold Ayl up, Keller came to a halt beside her. 'What—'

'Ssshhh!' Dray interrupted. 'Listen.'

Coming from the junction in the corridor up ahead was a faint sound. A soft pattering, almost like rain on a metal roof.

'Wait here.'

Before Keller had a chance to protest, Dray jogged towards the junction and peered round. The corridor

41

ahead was empty, but the noise was growing louder now. As she listened, the gentleness disappeared and it became a fast skittering noise. Screeches broke out – a twisted mix of a shekra-hawk's cry and the sound of metal being shredded.

Then something clicked in Dray's mind. It wasn't just a noise getting louder – it was something getting *closer*. The thought had hardly entered her brain when the first shape appeared at the far end of the corridor. She froze.

At first glance, it seemed to be some sort of insect, but it was easily as big as her. Six long double-jointed legs supported a multi-segmented body that bulged with barely constrained energy. Two long, twitching antennae were joined to the torso just above a pair of thick, whip-like arms, each with a mass of razor-sharp spikes on the end. Huge fanged mandibles ground against each other, oozing green liquid. Above them were the eyes – dozens of them – dark masses focused squarely on her.

Dray felt as if every drop of blood in her body had been replaced by pure terror. For a moment, her mind went blank. Then her training kicked in as she assessed the scene. Already, more of the alien creatures were moving up behind the first. The lead alien chittered softly and its fellows stopped, staring at her with their monstrous eye-clusters.

'Dray?' Keller called weakly.

'Stay back,' Dray replied, forcing the words out, though her throat was suddenly as dry as the surface of Bellus.

'What's that noise?'

'You don't want to know.' Without taking her eyes off the monsters before her, Dray started to slowly walk backwards. 'Go back inside.'

'But—'

'*Just do it!*'

From the corner of her eye, Dray saw Keller start to pull Ayl towards the banqueting hall. In front of her, the aliens held their ground, like soldiers waiting for the order to charge. For a moment, time seemed to stand still.

Then, with a sickening shriek, they raced towards her.

6

'Get in there now!'

Keller looked up to see Dray sprinting towards him. He barely had time to register the wall of clattering, shrieking noise that seemed to fill the corridor behind her before the Bellori girl slammed into him and Ayl, sending them flying back into the banqueting hall.

Spinning around, Dray hit the emergency seal button. The double-strength bulkhead slammed and locked into place, cutting off the ear-piercing cacophony. In the sudden silence, all Keller could hear was Dray panting as she fought to slow her breathing back to normal. Ayl lay on the floor where he had fallen, unmoving.

'Guard the door,' said Dray. 'They were just coming round the corner.'

'*They?*' asked Keller. 'Who are *they?*'

'I don't know. Aliens. I've never seen anything like them before.'

There was a strange note in Dray's voice. For a moment, Keller wondered if that was what it sounded like when a Bellori was scared.

'Aliens?' he echoed. 'Hostile?'

Dray looked at him as if he had three heads. 'What do you think?'

She turned away, pressing her com-link again and again. 'Krack!' she cursed. 'Nothing.'

'Well, what are we going to do?'

'How about we start by letting me think!' Dray paced up and down for a moment. 'We have to get out of here and reach the others.'

'Then why don't we try *that* door?' asked Keller, pointing at the exit on the other side of the room.

Dray shook her head. 'Even if they aren't already outside, we won't get far without weapons.'

'And what are you planning to use as weapons?' said Keller, waving his arm to indicate the deserted banqueting hall. 'Knives and forks?'

'No,' replied Dray. 'This.'

And with that, she placed her hands on either side of her head and wrenched it sharply to the left with a sickening crack.

Keller felt his stomach turn over.

She's killed herself, he thought. *Whatever she saw out*

there, it's driven her mad.

Dray's head had turned almost 180 degrees, as if she was looking back over her own shoulder. A narrow crack had appeared at the base of her neck, between the collar plates, but instead of blood, a faint light began to seep from it. It spread in two lines, one going along her arms, the other down the middle of her chest. It split again at the base of her torso, spreading down her legs.

Keller fell back, his eyes almost popping out of his head. What the hell was happening to her?

A loud hiss erupted, reminding him of pressure equalizing in an airlock. Then Dray's plates started to peel back, folding in segments along the routes the light had followed. Each slab made a clunking noise as it swung open. Finally, the Bellori pulled off her head – no, not her head, a *helmet* – and let it drop to the ground, and Keller felt his jaw drop with it.

Stepping out of the huge suit of armour plates that, until thirty clicks ago, Keller had thought was her skin, was a girl wearing a black one-piece combat overall. She was short – tiny compared to how bulky she had been before – but she had two legs, two arms, pink skin, and dark hair plaited flat against her head. She could have been a Cantorian. A fit, athletic Cantorian, but still…

Keller's mind reeled.

'I thought—'

'That we were a race of giants?' finished Dray.

'Well . . . yeah.'

'Misdirection,' said Dray. 'First rule of war. Who's going to pick a fight with the Bellori when we look like that?'

Keller could tell that his face was locked in an expression of total disbelief, but try as he might, he couldn't force it back to normal. Beside him, Ayl looked even more incredulous, if that were possible. Dray's transformation seemed to have shocked him out of his trance, and he was staring at her as if the worlds didn't make sense any more.

'Dray?' he gasped.

'You're back with us. Good. Give me a hand over here. You –' she gestured to Keller, 'keep an eye on the door.'

Dray turned back to her armour, quickly unclipping several objects from the inside. Spreading them out on one of the tables, she started snapping the pieces together. Moving like a sleepwalker under her direction, Ayl passed her more components as the seemingly random collection of parts started to come together.

Glad of the opportunity to compose himself, Keller made his way over to the door and pressed his ear to the metal. He couldn't hear anything, but he could feel a faint vibration against his cheek, as if something were scraping against the other side.

'Er, I think we need to get out of here,' he told the others, backing into the centre of the room. Behind him, Dray gave a satisfied grunt. Keller turned to see her holding some kind of gun, which was almost as big as she was. Three thick tubes were clasped together, a dark gunmetal stock attached at one end, with what looked like a firing mechanism underneath. Keller hadn't come into contact with many weapons on Cantor, but he'd seen enough to know that he was looking at a serious piece of kit.

'You smuggled in a kinetic shotgun?' he said, whistling. 'I'm impressed.'

Ayl looked up from the table in horror. 'I just helped you build a *weapon*?' he squeaked. 'This is a holy place. We're supposed to be at a peace conference!'

Dray ignored him.

'A warrior never goes unarmed,' she said. 'This is a Bellori's last defence. No one is ever supposed to see us without our armour.' She brought up the weapon until it was levelled at Keller's chest, and he suddenly realized that even without her armour on, the Bellori girl was still every inch a fighter.

'By rights, I should kill you right now,' Dray continued. 'But somehow I don't think it would be good for diplomatic relations. Believe me, though, if you *ever* breathe a word of this to anyone, I'll kill you then. That goes for you too, fish-boy.'

Ayl nodded weakly.

'Fine,' Keller agreed, smiling with a confidence he didn't quite feel. 'Let's just concentrate on staying alive first. We can discuss who gets to kill who later.'

Alum na ve rah sooo . . . Alum na ve rah sooo . . . Alum na ve rah sooo . . .

Ayl chanted the prayer over and over, but even the holy words couldn't disguise the echoing emptiness in his mind. Since the moment the connection to his mother had been broken, Ayl had been reaching out, frantically searching for her, but without success. He couldn't reach the minds of any of the other Aquanth delegates either. It felt like a door had been slammed in his face. He was finally alone with his thoughts, and he didn't like it one bit.

'So what do we do now?' he asked, trying to keep the fear out of his voice.

'We go and find everyone else.' Dray narrowed her eyes and jogged over to the exit on the far side of the room. Standing back from it, she nodded to Keller.

Ayl held his breath as the trade prince reached for the control. If the aliens had already reached this door too, they were trapped.

Dray clenched her jaw. 'Open it.'

Keller pressed the control. With a hiss, the door unsealed. Beyond, the corridor was empty.

Without hesitating, Dray stepped through, scanning for the enemy.

'Clear,' she called. 'Come on.'

Ayl shot a nervous look at Keller. He was still leaning against the wall, trying to look nonchalant, but Ayl could sense the Cantorian's fear and uncertainty. Dray had already disappeared from view.

'I suppose we'd better stick together,' he said finally.

Keller sighed. 'Yeah,' he said. 'Come on then.'

The corridor was the same as all the others in the facility. Bare metal walls stretched up to the ceiling, punctuated by maintenance hatches and air ducts every few paces. The light panels still flashed red, casting intimidating shadows on the deck-plating.

The three of them walked along, not speaking. Ayl wished they could talk, just to fill the silence in his head. He felt so alone. Was this what it was like for them all the time? It was terrifying.

Dray seemed comfortable enough, striding ahead in the lead, sweeping the gun around as though it was an extension of her arms. Her confidence had been growing ever since she had got hold of the weapon. Ayl still felt queasy that his hands had helped construct a tool of death, but he had to admit he did feel safer now she had it.

'Do you actually know where we're going?' asked Keller suddenly, his voice sounding dangerously loud in the empty corridor.

'Of course,' growled Dray.

'Just that this corridor looks very familiar . . .'

Dray spun on her heel, squaring up to Keller. The move would have been menacing if she had still been wearing her armour, but didn't have quite the same effect now that she was a full head shorter than he was. Ayl wasn't sure that she realized that yet, though.

'Look, Cantorian, if you think you can find a better route, just say.'

The taller boy stiffened. 'My *name* is Keller,' he snapped. 'And a blind swamp rat could find a better route than you.'

'Why, you arrogant little—'

Ayl turned away as the angry voices rose. Couldn't

they stop arguing for five minutes? He could feel all the pent-up emotions inside him turning into frustration, building like a tidal wave until he couldn't take it any more.

'Look, just *shut up*!'

Silence.

Dray and Keller turned to stare at him, their mouths open in surprise. Ayl stared back, hardly able to believe he had just shouted for the first time in his life.

And then they heard it.

Faint at first, a tapping and scraping coming from somewhere behind them.

Dray raised the k-gun up to her shoulder. 'Listen.'

A loud clang made Ayl jump. 'It's coming this way.'

'Where is it?' asked Keller, swinging around. 'I can't see anything.'

Another grinding scrape, even closer this time. Dray tracked the sound with her weapon. 'Oh krack,' she cursed. 'They're in the walls. Run!'

'Too late,' said Keller, as the scrabbling noise passed right by them. 'Look.'

One of the air duct covers just ahead of them burst out of its housing and clattered against the opposite wall. Two long antennae flicked out of the hole, searching around the corridor. Ayl backed away as a writing mass of long, jointed legs sprouted through the opening. The limbs strained with a tremendous strength as their claws dug into the surrounding metal and a huge, bulbous body started to squeeze through the gap.

With a shriek of protest, the metal gave way and the creature burst through, tumbling to the ground. For an instant, the tangled mess of insect body parts scrabbled on the floor, trying to right itself. Then, in a blur of sharp movements, it sprang upright.

Ayl stared in horror. He had almost managed to convince himself that the glimpse he had caught through his mother's eyes, as these creatures had burst into the conference chamber, had been a mistake. A hallucination. But now it stood before him, like some hideous crustacean from the darkest depths.

And he suddenly realized that he wasn't alone in his mind any more.

Dray aimed her k-gun right between the alien's eye-clusters, her focus total as she took the measure of her enemy.

Taller than she was, its body covered in natural armour, the alien had no obvious weaknesses. It was almost like facing off with Garal again. Except her sparring partner's eyes had never glittered with such hungry malevolence.

As the alien stared at her, Dray shivered as she felt the air move against her skin. For the first time she realized how vulnerable she was without her own armour on. Instead of scratching her armour, those claws could dig deep into her body. One swipe of those long, whip-like arms could rip the flesh from her bones . . .

Concentrate! she told herself angrily, snapping her attention back to the enemy. *Don't get distracted.*

But it was hard to focus when already she could hear the *tap-tap-tapping* of claws as another of the insect-creatures pulled itself out of the hole torn by its leader. Dray took a deep breath, a horrible realization slowly dawning. Even with the k-gun there was no way that they were going to be able to fight their way through to the conference chamber. There were just too many of these creatures, and only one of her. She had a feeling the prince might just be able to hold his own in a fight, but he was unarmed, and Ayl was worse than useless. The only option was to retreat.

As if sensing her weakness, the lead creature leaned back, legs bending so its body nearly rested on the ground. Then its legs snapped forward, launching the alien through the air towards her, its outstretched arms reaching for her face.

Wumph!

Dray pulled the trigger and the creature's body dissolved into a thick yellow ichor that flowed down the corridor. Its arms, legs and antennae rattled against the walls and fell to the floor. They twitched for a click, then went still.

'Change of plan,' Dray yelled. 'Follow me!'

Keller ran until he thought his lungs would melt. Ahead of him, Dray was pulling away. He chanced a glance back the way they had come. Ayl was five paces behind him, and twenty paces behind that a swarm of the alien creatures skittered along, their legs a grotesque blur of movement.

Krack, he thought. *They're gaining.*

He forced his legs to move faster, wishing he hadn't eaten quite so much at the banquet. But how was he supposed to know he'd be running for his life barely an hour later?

'Come on, Ayl!' he screamed.

Behind him, the creatures' nerve-shredding chittering had risen to fever pitch, punctuated by screeches as they bore down on their prey. Keller knew they could never outrun these six-legged horrors. Their only chance was to find some sort of barrier.

Even as he thought it, Keller spotted the circular

opening in the wall.

'Dray!' he yelled. 'Go left! NOW!'

Dray turned without hesitation, hurdling the low threshold, and a moment later Keller stumbled through the opening behind her. He spun round. Ayl was right behind them, but the monsters were just behind *him*. The lashing whip-arm of the leading creature was just millipaces from his head.

'Jump!' barked Dray.

Eyes bulging with terror, Ayl leaped forward, tumbling through the doorway. Keller slammed his palm on to the emergency lock panel and the door irised shut.

Keller slumped over in relief and fought to catch his breath. 'That was too close,' he gasped. 'What in the name of Trinity are those things?'

'Aliens,' panted Ayl. 'The same ones who broke into the conference chamber. They're trying to break in here too.'

'What are you talking about, temple-boy?' Dray growled, her voice hoarse. 'That's ten millipaces of reinforced deuterium. Nothing is coming through that door. We are as safe here as . . .'

Dray's voice trailed off as something started pounding against the door. A lone, rhythmic beating at first, the noise rose to become a cacophony of drumming. A moment later, the first dents started to appear.

'Safe?' Keller spluttered.

The Aquanth's eyes were wide, but he was weirdly still. 'They won't leave us. They'll batter at the door until they break through.'

Dray scowled. 'How do you know that?'

'I can hear them,' whispered Ayl. 'In my mind. Hear their voices.'

Keller stared at the blue-skinned boy. Maybe he'd taken one too many knocks to the head today. But one thing couldn't be denied – the aliens were breaking through. Already, the metal had started to buckle, the hardened material bending under the intense force of their blows.

'We need to get out of here,' said Keller. 'I recognize this corridor. It leads to the space hangar. If we can get there, we can get on to my ship.'

'But isn't the conference chamber the other way?' Ayl asked.

Keller exchanged a look with Dray and her face twisted uncomfortably. She must have come to the same conclusion that he had.

'Tactically, a retreat is the best course of action,' she admitted gruffly. 'There is no dishonour.'

Ayl shook his head. 'But we can't go without our parents. I mean—'

'Listen, Ayl,' said Keller urgently. 'We don't stand a chance against that horde. And if our parents have been . . . captured, our planets aren't prepared, not for a surprise attack like this. We have to warn the home worlds.' He stared into Ayl's eyes.

'If we don't get out now,' the trade prince went on, 'the home worlds are next.'

Ayl could hear the others talking. He could hear Keller explaining why it was right to abandon their parents, and Dray talking about tactics and honour, but their words were like waves on the surface, and he was deep underwater. There were stronger sounds here. The chittering of a hundred voices, thousands. And they were moving towards him, towards *them*. Fast.

'They're coming!' he gasped.

'We need to go,' snapped Dray, breaking into a run.

Ayl stumbled after her. He felt an arm around his shoulders and realized Keller was supporting him, hurrying him along as Dray raced down the corridor ahead of them. He watched her with fascination. Almost everything she did went against the divine principles that ruled Aquanth life – yet without her, he'd be dead. Her body was relaxed, every muscle ready. The weapon hung loosely in her hands but seemed so much a part of her. She was full of a calm, controlled rage. He felt his mind reach out to her, to try to share that calm, and he recoiled in shock.

I just tried to mind-share with a Bellori, he thought in horror. Being alone in his head must have made him crazier than he'd realized.

Not that he was truly alone. His head was filled with the creatures' noise. The sound of their minds crying out in triumph.

'They're through the door!' he cried.

Ayl tried to run faster, but the webbed feet that propelled him so smoothly through the water were awkward and clumsy on land. Suddenly the air-vent grilles flew away from the walls behind them and a stream of the alien creatures burst through into the corridor. Something caught the collar of Ayl's tunic, yanking him backwards. He stumbled and fell, hard. Above him loomed one of the aliens, its fangs gleaming with venom.

This is it, thought Ayl. *Death*.

Then another figure stood over him. Dray. She fired her weapon before Ayl had time to catch his breath. The alien somersaulted backwards, its body shattered by the k-gun's blast.

'Get him out of here, Keller!' screamed Dray. 'I've got your backs.'

Ayl felt his arm almost wrenched out of its socket as the Cantorian pulled him to his feet, and they broke into a run once more.

The bugs were stampeding down the passage now. They crawled and ran along the floor, the walls, the ceiling. The swarm covered every surface. Dray raised the k-gun again and blew another of the foremost ones apart. Alien body parts showered those behind in thick yellow blood as she fired again and again. Tangled masses of bodies and serrated legs heaped up as the insects furiously tried to force a way through.

Keller and Ayl were already at the next turning. Dray turned and sprinted towards them, feeling the adrenaline course through her veins as she realized how much quicker she was without her armour. She felt so fast! *Fast, but not as strong*, she reminded herself grimly.

'It's not far,' Keller called. 'Come on!'

They made it to the next corridor, closing another door behind them. The swarm screeched in frustration as it slammed into the barrier.

'That won't hold them for long,' Dray snapped.

'Where's the hangar?'

'Just through here. We've made it!' Keller jogged to a door a few paces away and palmed the airlock release panel.

Nothing happened.

He slammed his hand against the control again.

'It's locked!' He groaned, a look of panic overtaking his usual smug expression.

'Well, get it unlocked then!' barked Dray.

Fumbling in his pocket, Keller pulled out his data-slate and started urgently thumbing the screen.

'What are you doing?' yelled Dray. 'You haven't got time to read the kracking manual!'

Ignoring her jibe, Keller tapped in a five-digit code and the reader folded open like a book, revealing a tangle of wire and a set of controls. He ran the thin cable to the wall and attached it with a magnet.

Dray snorted. 'You're a hacker?'

'You're not the only one with hidden depths, Dray,' Keller retorted. 'I can get us through here, but I'm going to need some time.'

Dray nodded, turned and walked back up the corridor, priming her weapon.

The first bug came round the corner. Dray lifted the weapon and the insect was blown apart, splattering the wall in gore. More came, crawling on the walls and the ceiling. She took her time and aimed, hitting each one perfectly. But for every one that was killed, five more appeared around the bend. The corridor soon became one solid mass of bugs, covering every surface, crawling over each other – a living wall of chittering and screeching. Every sledgehammer blow from the k-gun made a dent, slowed them down, but more and more came forwards.

'Quickly, Keller . . .' Dray warned. She was practically standing on top of them now.

'Got it!' Keller cried, and the door spiralled open.

'Now!'

Keller and Ayl scrambled through the airlock, rushing to get out of the way. Dray fired a quick volley of shots and dived after them, rolling and spinning round to face the enemy again before sending out two more blasts.

The first shot smashed directly into the closest bugs, creating a squirming barricade of body parts that blocked the way for those beyond.

The second shot hit the airlock controls. Sparks burst from the wall and the door slammed shut.

Keller looked round at the hangar. They'd come through

here only a few hours before. It had seemed full of energy when it was packed with delegates. Now it was deserted. The flags and banners of the three Trinity worlds hung dismally from the ceiling. The red carpets still led from the ships. Where there had been noise and clamour before, now there was a ghostly silence.

'This way,' he said, leading them quickly towards the sleek Cantorian vessel. Bounding up the boarding ramp, Keller made straight for the flight deck, with the other two right behind. 'Strap yourselves in,' he called out. 'This might get a bit bumpy.'

He jumped into the pilot's chair and immediately flickering display panels came to life. A soft, genderless voice greeted them, seeming to come from all directions at once.

'Hello, Keller. I hope your stay was pleasurable.'

'Ship, this is an emergency. Get the engines to optimal and open the hangar doors,' Keller barked, his fingers dancing over the control console.

'Understood. One moment please.'

'Are you sure you know what you're doing?' said Dray's voice from behind him. It seemed that the Bellori didn't like someone else calling the shots – or firing them.

'I've won the Zorax Cup six turns in a row,' Keller

said, smirking. 'I think I can manage a Class 2 cruiser. I'm patching you through to the scanners, so if you don't mind keeping an eye on things outside, I'll get on with saving our lives.'

He tapped the console and a series of screens folded out from the wall behind him, showing live feeds from cameras all over the ship's hull.

'All right, no need to be a mullock about it,' growled Dray, turning to the screens. 'Oh, krack!'

'What?' Keller turned just in time to see the airlock door burst open. The creatures started to stream through, charging straight for the cruiser.

'They're in,' Dray said.

'Ship, get those hangar doors open now!' shouted Keller.

'Affirmative. Hangar doors opening.'

The main view-screen showed the huge doors sliding open, revealing a tantalizing glimpse of stars beyond. Keller's hands clasped the controls.

'Warning!' chimed the ship. 'Engines are not fully operational. Inertial dampeners not at full capacity. Warning!'

'Like I said, it's going to be bumpy.'

Keller pulled back on the control column. The acceleration rammed them back into their seats, and the ship leaped forwards, out of the bay into space.

And stopped.

'Engine failure. Repeat: engine failure. Activating diagnostics and auto-repair,' the ship calmly intoned.

Keller swore. 'Give me a minute . . .' His eyes ran over the displays, trying to get a picture of what was happening.

Beside him, Ayl was sitting with his knees up to his chest, his slender arms wrapped around them. It was as close to the foetal position as anyone could get in a flight seat. '*Alum na ve rah sooo . . . Alum na ve rah sooo . . .*' the Aquanth murmured.

'We're safe,' said Keller with relief. 'We're drifting about five hundred paces outside the hangar. I just need to get the engines started again and—'

'We've got trouble,' barked Dray. 'The bugs – they're following us!'

'What?' Keller turned to look at the screen.

Dozens of the creatures were launching themselves from the hangar's walls, propelling themselves off the surface of the asteroid, claws snapping as they flew.

Keller stared, disbelievingly. 'That's impossible – it's a vacuum out there!'

'Tell that to them!' Dray yelled, stabbing her finger into the screen.

Keller heard Ayl let out a low whimper as a dull clank echoed through the ship. Then there was another, and another.

Then the screens went blank.

8

'Warning: primary sensors offline,' said the ship. 'Damage to outer hull.'

'What does it mean?' Ayl cried as the sound of shrieking metal filled the cabin.

'It means we're in trouble.' Keller's hands flew over the controls. 'Switch to auxiliary sensors,' he shouted. 'Get those engines working.'

'Please wait,' the ship said.

A moment later, the screens in front of Ayl flickered back to life, showing the outside of the cruiser from a different angle. He cringed in terror. Outside, dozens of giant insects swarmed over the hull. Their long, serrated arms were driving into the metal and tearing great chunks of plating away, like a pack of harun-fins savaging the body of a chi-whale in a vicious feeding frenzy. The once-smooth outer skin of the ship was already tattered and scarred.

'We need to fight back,' yelled Dray. 'What weapons systems does this ship have?'

'This is a trade craft,' Keller replied tersely, his eyes still on the displays in front of him. 'It's unarmed.'

Dray swore loudly. 'You mean we're *defenceless*?'

'We didn't come here to fight a war!' screamed Keller.

Ayl shrank back in his seat. Couldn't the other two see that fighting each other wasn't going to help? They needed to be calm. Taking a deep breath, he began to chant again.

'*Alum na ve rah sooo . . . Alum na ve rah sooo . . .*'

It seemed to work. Both Keller and Dray stopped yelling and turned to stare at him.

'What are you doing, fish-boy?' snarled Dray.

'Clearing my mind,' replied Ayl. 'There must be another way to escape, but we won't find it by shouting. We need to rely on ourselves, not weapons of war.'

'That's it!' said Keller, slapped his forehead with his palm. 'The main engines aren't the only way to move a ship. Ship, give me manoeuvring thrusters.'

'Thrusters online,' replied the emotionless voice.

'Activate emergency restraints.'

'Activating.'

Ayl felt an iron grip settle across his chest as a mesh of light beams sprang from the sides of his flight seat.

'What are you doing, Cantorian?' growled Dray, struggling in the next chair. 'Let me go!'

'That really wouldn't be advisable,' said Keller with a grim smile. 'Brace yourselves.'

Setting his jaw, he thumbed a button on the arm of his own flight seat. With a tortured engine-howl, the ship leapt forward.

Ayl was slammed backwards by an unseen hand. He glanced over at Keller and Dray, G-force pushing at their faces, stretching their cheeks and foreheads. He felt as if his insides had been left behind on the asteroid. He wanted to clamp his eyelids shut and block out the images on the view-screen, but the force kept them pinned open. Most of the aliens seemed to have fallen away from the hull, thrown by the ship's sudden burst of speed, but several were still clinging on.

'It's not working,' Dray said from between gritted teeth.

'Not yet,' replied Keller, pressing another button.

Ayl couldn't help moaning as the ship began to spin. It was slow at first, but soon picked up speed until the world became a blur. It was like being trapped in a whirlpool, endlessly corkscrewing round and round. But through his rising nausea, he could see the remaining aliens slipping off one by one to be caught in the superheated exhaust trail of the ship's thrusters and incinerated.

'Stop!' Dray called out. 'They're gone.'

Keller tapped another key, and the ship abruptly righted itself. As the beams of the emergency restraints glimmered and then faded to nothing, he turned and grinned.

'Thank you for flying Cantor Spaceways. We hope you had a pleasant trip and we apologize for any turbulence . . .'

Before he could finish, Ayl stood up, swayed, then fell to his knees and spewed partially-digested seaweed from all three of his stomachs.

Dray recoiled with a snort of disgust. Trust an Aquanth not to be able to take a little high-G manoeuvring.

'I'm sorry,' said Ayl, as he lifted himself weakly into his seat again. 'This is only my second journey in a spaceship.'

'Yeah, well just try to avoid the seats, OK?' said Keller. 'They're Grade A quantook leather.'

'I'll try,' Ayl promised.

'We haven't got time to worry about interior decorating,' snapped Dray. 'Cantorian, give me communications, now.'

'No can do, *chief*,' replied Keller, looking over the control console. 'Those bugs have ripped up the coms-dish.'

'Then plot us a course to the nearest inhabited outpost,' ordered Dray, standing up. 'I'll go out and make repairs.'

'You're going to spacewalk on the hull of a moving vessel?' Keller's eyes bulged in disbelief. 'Are you crazy?'

Dray fixed him with a flat stare. 'No. I am Bellori.'

She turned and walked off the bridge, scanning the rest of the cruiser. For all its flashy gadgets and pointless luxuries, it was laid out much like a Bellori warship. In an emergency, everyone wanted a quick escape route, and Dray found what she needed in a cupboard next to the airlock in the main compartment.

Pulling out a silver spacesuit, she couldn't help but marvel at how limited it seemed compared to the armour she'd worn her entire life. Bellori battle plates were airtight and climate controlled, able to work under water or in the void of space, as well as protecting its wearer from most forms of weapon. This flimsy Cantorian suit wouldn't stand up to a single laser beam – but, she grudgingly admitted, it would do the job she needed it for now. Like everything else on the Cantorian vessel, it was a top-of-the-line model.

With the suit on and the helmet secure, she stepped

into the airlock and activated the decompression control.

'Dray, can you hear me?'

'What the—' Dray winced as the Cantorian's voice crackled too loudly through a speaker near her ear. 'I thought you said communications were disabled.'

'This is the internal network, just to the suit. I've laid in a course.'

'Then let's get going,' barked Dray. 'And quickly. I'll be back in five.'

Not for the first time, she cursed her luck. Here she was, in a genuine combat situation, the one thing she had always dreamed about. But this wasn't the glorious battle of her fantasies. This was a hasty retreat from an unknown enemy, babysitting two useless civilians. Maybe not *entirely* useless. The Cantorian seemed to be a good pilot. But as for that waste-of-space fish-boy . . .

The light above the airlock went from red to green and the heavy door slid aside. She stood for a moment, staring out into deep space, then stepped out into the vacuum, her magnetized boots locking on to the metal hull.

The ship had looked in bad enough shape through the sensor screens. Now that she was making her way across the scarred metal, however, Dray could appreciate the full scale of the damage. Almost a third of the plating had been torn away, and most of what remained was scarred and cracked. And the creatures had done this with their bare hands – bare *claws*, she corrected herself with a shudder. Even a Bellori battleship would have struggled to take this sort of damage. Whatever else these aliens might be, they were formidable warriors.

Loose wires crackled, sending streamers of sparks fizzing off into space, and long scorch marks showed where the ship's own plasma exhaust had struck the hull during their desperate spin. Luckily, the coms-dish hadn't been entirely ripped away. It hung loose, close to the airlock door, stuck between two jagged angles of carbotanium plate. Clumping over, Dray began cutting through a piece of the hull with a mini-blowtorch to free it.

After a minute that felt like forever, the metal snapped free. Working quickly, Dray fixed the coms-dish back into place. It was battered and dented, but intact. The wires connecting it to the main ship, though, were frayed and tattered. Dray frowned. She wasn't enough of an electronics expert to know if the system would still work. They could only try.

The hull of the ship began to vibrate slightly beneath Dray's feet. The Cantorian must have engaged the engines. It was time to get inside. Despite her bravado, Dray knew it was foolish to be space walking on a moving vessel if you didn't have to be. Tucking away the blowtorch, she turned back towards the airlock.

And found herself face to face with an alien.

Keller leaned back in his flight seat and stretched. Every muscle in his body ached. When this was all over, he was going to take a *long* holiday.

Beside him, Ayl was trying to mop up the seaweed-scented puddle on the floor of the bridge.

'Just leave it,' Keller said. 'I don't know about you, but I need to relax.'

Getting to his feet, Keller headed for the living compartment.

'Shouldn't you be flying the ship?' Ayl gasped, looking up from the floor.

'It's on auto,' replied Keller, rolling his eyes. 'This ship is more than capable of looking after itself.'

Ayl nodded, scrambling to his feet and putting one of his hands in the pool of vomit in the process. Keller sighed. 'Unlike some.'

'What about Dray?' asked the blue-skinned boy,

following him into the living compartment.

'What about her?' Keller shot back, throwing himself into an overstuffed floating chair. 'She's probably out there chewing plutonium rods, or whatever it is the Bellori do for fun.'

'But shouldn't she have finished by now?' Ayl's long hands fluttered nervously.

As if in answer, the airlock chimed.

'Here she comes,' said Keller. 'Let's hope she's in a better mood.'

The airlock door hissed open and Dray staggered into the compartment.

Keller leapt to his feet with a cry of alarm. The Bellori girl was barely visible beneath the tangle of insectoid legs wrapped around her body. She was off balance, wrestling with the creature as if she was trying to keep its claws from her throat. Taking two short steps, Dray fell backwards, hitting the deck with a heavy thump, the monstrous creature landing on top of her.

Keller felt his limbs freeze with terror. Beside him, Ayl screamed.

Dray stuck her head out from beneath the giant body. 'I'm back.'

'But . . . But . . . It's one of the . . .' stammered Ayl,

both sets of eyelids opening wide. 'It'll kill us all!'

'Calm down,' said Dray, fixing the Aquanth with a withering look. 'It's dead.'

Keller could see that she was right. The alien was cut almost in half along its centre, all but one of the legs on the left side still intact, the right side a mass of burnt shell and flesh.

'Now stop gawping and get this thing off me!'

Forcing his feet into action, Keller staggered over to the alien. Its gleaming carapace was cold and smooth to the touch, so smooth it was hard to get a grip on it. Grabbing one of the leg joints, he heaved.

Even with half its body missing, the creature was still heavy. Keller groaned as he pulled with all his strength. With Dray pushing from beneath, they finally managed to roll the alien off her body and on to the floor. The Bellori jumped smartly to her feet and Keller looked her up and down. She didn't seem to be injured, but her spacesuit was covered with sticky yellow blood. The rancid smell filled his nostrils.

Ayl was staring at the dead creature with wide eyes. Keller hoped he wasn't about to be sick again. Dray just wiped the worst of the blood off her hands and started to strip off her spacesuit. 'Report,' she barked.

'What?'

'Report,' Dray repeated. 'What's happening?'

'I think *you* should be telling *us*,' said Keller. 'Is that really one of the aliens?'

'Affirmative,' said Dray. 'Half of one anyway. It was caught in the thruster vents. You shook it loose when you restarted the engines. Unfortunately, it was already dead.'

'Did you say *un*fortunately?' asked Keller. 'Why, did you want to kill it yourself?'

Dray glared at him. 'You can learn more from a prisoner than a corpse, Cantorian. Information is valuable. These creatures are a formidable enemy.'

'I'll say,' Keller agreed. He nudged the alien with a boot. 'But nothing the Bellori can't handle, right?'

'If we strike hard and fast, perhaps,' Dray replied. 'They don't seem to be particularly intelligent. But they are strong and ferocious, and we don't know how many of them there are. In sufficient numbers, they could overwhelm an army. Perhaps even a whole planet.'

Keller's mind was suddenly filled with an image of thousands of the aliens swarming over Cantor like a plague of giant loci-pests, scrambling over the Trade Hall with their jagged, thorny legs, ripping apart anyone who stood in their way.

Ayl grabbed his arm. 'Yes,' he whispered, as if he had

been reading Keller's thoughts. 'We need to warn our people before they attack our homes.'

'Did you manage to repair the coms-dish?'

Dray nodded. 'But I don't know whether it will be fully functional. We should—'

Without warning, a harsh, scratchy voice sounded through the ship's speakers.

'Unidentified vessel, this is restricted space. Identify yourself immediately or we will open fire.'

Keller pursed his lips. 'Seems functional enough to me.'

The trio ran back towards the bridge.

'Who was that?' asked Ayl.

Keller shrugged. 'I don't know, but they sounded a lot like *her*.'

Dray stabbed at the communications panel. 'This is Dray, daughter of General Iccus, commanding Cantorian cruiser ID alpha-alpha-alpha-zero-zero-two. I must speak to your captain immediately.'

'Commanding?' asked Keller, raising an eyebrow.

Before Dray could respond, a new voice came over the speaker.

'This is Sudor, acting commander of the *Astyanax*. Why are you not at your father's side?'

'Sudor, pay attention: the conference has been

attacked by aliens,' said Dray. 'My father is a captive. I have the heirs to Cantor and Aquanthis with me. No one else escaped—'

'What aliens?' interrupted Sudor. 'Our sensors detected no attacking ships.'

'Well they're there,' insisted Dray. 'We must send a warning message to Cantor and Aquanthis, and then attack the asteroid immediately.'

A moment's silence followed. Then Sudor's voice came through again. 'In the absence of General Iccus, I am assuming command of the battle fleet. You have no authority—'

'What?' Dray's face flushed an ugly red. 'You can't just take over! We have to warn the other planets!'

'. . . to give orders. No message will be sent. You will be brought on-board and returned to Bellus . . .'

'Listen to her!' shouted Keller. The Bellori's voice carried on as though he hadn't spoken.

'. . . where you will be questioned by the Admiralty Council, which will determine the proper strategy . . .'

'Sudor, you mullock,' hissed Dray. 'There's no time for that!'

'This communication is over.'

The channel cut out.

9

Dray was almost thrown from her seat when the ship lurched, as if bumped by a giant fist.

'They've got us in a tractor beam,' she said, scanning the displays.

The trade prince's fingers danced over the flight controls. The engines whined, but the ship continued its slow turn. On the view-screen, a huge spaceship slowly came into view, bristling with weapons.

'The Bellori flagship,' hissed Keller. 'We're being pulled in . . .'

'What are we going to do?' said Ayl desperately. 'We have to warn the planets.'

Keller jumped up from his seat and rounded on Dray.

'What the krack is going on here?' he demanded, jabbing an accusing finger towards her. 'This is kidnapping! You people can't do this to me!'

Dray stood up slowly. The spoiled brat was blaming

her for this? She was a lot smaller than the Cantorian, but Sudor had created a huge reservoir of rage inside her, and now that rage had a target.

'Get back in your seat, fly-boy, before you make me hurt you.'

Keller bristled. 'I'm not some army dunce for you to command,' he snarled. 'I'm the Trade Prince of Cantor! You boneheaded Bellori can't just—'

'Don't call me bonehead!' roared Dray. Before she was even aware she was moving, she had snatched hold of Keller's hand and spun him round, twisting his arm behind his back.

The Cantorian cried out in pain. 'Get off!' he screamed.

'Make me!' Dray shouted back.

'STOP IT!'

Ayl leapt to his feet, his gills trembling with rage. 'An alien horde has attacked the three races. It has captured our parents. Our homes are threatened. And you two are squabbling like hatchling loci-fish!'

He closed both sets of eyelids for a moment, as if he was calming himself. Then he looked directly at Dray and pointed a webbed finger at her. 'Let him go,' he said softly, but with the sort of authority Dray had only heard in her father's voice.

Dray released her hold on Keller, stepping back to give the trade prince room. She watched the Cantorian as he turned stiffly, rubbing and rolling his shoulder. She silently cursed herself. Her temper was always getting her into trouble. A warrior should have more control. There was nothing for it – she would have to apologize.

'I am . . . sorry,' said Dray. 'I should not have attacked you without warning. There is no honour in that.'

Keller chewed his lip. 'Yeah, well, I shouldn't have called you names. I'm sorry too.'

The two locked eyes for a moment, and Dray noticed something in Keller's gaze she hadn't seen there before. Respect.

'So,' said the trade prince, with the hint of a smile. 'What's the plan then?'

'Dray,' said the Aquanth. 'These are your people. Can you not reason with them?'

'That was Sudor,' she replied. 'Captain of my father's special forces. He isn't known for being reasonable. Can the ship escape the tractor beam?'

'No chance,' said Keller. 'Even if the engines were at full capacity, we wouldn't have the power. And we took a lot of damage earlier.'

Dray ground her teeth. They were out of options. But even as she had the thought, her father's gruff voice filled her head, repeating one of his favourite sayings: *There's no such thing as a no-win situation* . . .

This situation was a puzzle; no different to the tactical problems her father was so fond of setting her. And the key to solving those was always simple – work with the tools you actually have, not the ones you wish you did.

She looked first at Ayl, then at Keller. What skills did they have that could help here? Dray's heart leapt.

'I know how we can turn off the beam!' she exclaimed. 'Keller, you can hack into the battleship's computer.'

Keller snorted. 'Uh, it's not that easy, chief. Remote-hacking a Bellori battleship isn't like opening a locked door. Without the right security codes, I won't even be able to get a link.'

'Well here's a bit of luck,' said Dray, with a rare smile. She couldn't quite believe what she was about to do. It was reckless, treacherous and it would drive Sudor mad with fury.

In short, it was perfect.

'It just so happens that I know the codes.'

* * *

For a moment, Keller just stared at her. Then he laughed out loud.

'Well, why didn't you just say so?' He leapt back into his seat and started typing rapidly on a console. 'This shouldn't take five clicks . . .'

'That's just as well,' replied Dray, 'seeing as we don't *have* five clicks.'

But Keller barely heard her. He was entirely focused on the programme he was writing. A fierce emotion filled him, different from any kind he had felt before. It wasn't the same as when he had duped Tyrus, or even when he was racing. Those situations were exciting, but deep down he always knew he could win. Now he was playing for higher stakes – perhaps the safety of his whole planet. He'd always thought that responsibility was dull, a burden, something to be avoided. Now he was beginning to realize it could be quite the opposite.

'There!' He finished the final line and turned to Dray. 'If you don't mind, skipper.'

Leaning over the console, Dray tapped in a long string of numbers and letters. Keller held his breath.

A low chime sounded.

'Connection secure,' said the ship.

'Yes! Deactivate the tractor beam,' grinned Keller.

'Beam deactivated.'

Keller cried out in triumph. 'Resume previous course.'

'Resuming.'

The Bellori battleship disappeared from the view-screen as the cruiser turned back on to its previous path. Instantly, Sudor's deep voice boomed out of the speakers. 'How did you disable the beam? You will dock with us immediately or you will be condemned as criminals!'

Keller couldn't help himself. He turned and grinned at the others, then leaned in close to the microphone on the control console.

'Kiss my exhaust trail.' He laughed as his hand hit the engine ignition button. With a low roar, the cruiser leapt forward like a startled animal. 'Wooooo-hooooooo!' he yelled as they continued to accelerate. 'We're free!'

Dray spun her seat to look at the scanner screens. 'It's not going to be that easy, Keller.'

Keller studied the screen. The giant battleship was already turning on to their course. A click later, lasers flickered from the warship's prow.

'Warning!' said the ship. 'Energy weapon attack!'

'They're shooting at us?' Ayl bleated.

'What did you expect?' Dray barked. 'That they'd

just sit back and watch us go?'

The ship trembled as deflector shields absorbed the blast.

'That didn't seem so bad,' remarked Keller.

'They're not trying to destroy us,' said Dray. 'Just disable the engines. They'll wear us down and board us.'

'Warning!' said the ship as the lasers flashed again. 'Energy weapon attack! Defensive failure in two minutes.'

'I'm redirecting power to the deflectors,' said Keller. 'It might buy us some time.'

'Time for what?' snapped Dray. 'That's a Bellori battleship. It can outgun us and outrun us too.'

'If you've got any better suggestions, I'd love to hear them.'

Suddenly, Ayl stuck his head over their shoulders. 'If we can't fight and we can't run,' he said, 'let's hide instead.'

'Hide? Where?'

'There.' Ayl's slender finger picked out what looked like a faint, dusty smudge on the view-screen.

'What's that?' Keller winced as another laser blast rattled the ship.

'An asteroid field,' said Dray, turning to Ayl. 'What

use is that, fish-boy?'

'I am not a fish,' replied Ayl, his voice hard. 'But I do know that small ones use coral reefs to hide from bigger ones.'

Keller couldn't suppress a laugh as the confusion on Dray's face turned to disbelief. 'He's right – we can hide in there. The battleship is too big to follow us.'

Dray shook her head. 'As if this day wasn't weird enough already, now we're taking battle-tactics lessons from an Aquanth . . .'

'Never mind that,' said Keller. 'Let's just hope I can get us there in one piece. I'll tell you what, Ayl. You don't say much, but what you do say is pretty good.'

He grinned at the blue-skinned boy, who smiled back shyly.

'Warning!' said the ship again. 'Defensive failure in ninety clicks.'

'Ship, give me manoeuvring control,' said Keller.

'You have control, Keller.'

He took a deep breath. 'Hold on to your hats . . .'

Ayl gripped the arms of his flight seat as Keller swung the cruiser to starboard, evading another blast of laser fire, then pulled up hard, pointing the ship towards the asteroid field.

In his studies of Cantorian society, Ayl had read about something called 'zero-G racing', and how the young people of that planet enjoyed being thrown around in a machine designed to simulate the sensation of imminent death. He remembered thinking how absurd it sounded. How could a quick adrenaline rush ever compare to the deep, spiritual richness of quiet contemplation?

Now, though, as he shared the waves of exultation and excitement coming from Keller, and felt the pounding of his own heart, he was beginning to understand. His eyes were wide open and his mind felt sharp. He was terrified, yes, but exhilarated as well.

Ayl watched the stars in the forward viewing screen swing to the left as Keller dived to avoid a new Bellori attack. When they stopped turning, he could see that the vague dusty line that marked the edge of the asteroid field had grown thicker. The specks of dust were resolving themselves into dark dots, then tiny pebbles.

'We're almost there, Keller,' he shouted.

Suddenly, the ship was rocked by another volley of laser fire.

'Warning! Defensive failure in thirty clicks,' chimed the ship in its emotionless voice.

'What's happening, Dray?' shouted Keller. Ayl could

see the Cantorian's eyes fixed on the view-screen, his face lit up by electric lights shining in a dozen colours.

'They've guessed what we're trying to do,' Dray replied. 'They've increased the laser's power. They're trying to stop us before we get there.'

The ship rocked again, the engines groaning in protest.

'Warning! Defensive failure in ten clicks.'

'They're right on our tail!' Keller spun the cruiser in a wide arc, narrowly avoiding a second barrage.

Ayl could see the pebbles expanding rapidly now. One moment, they were the size of small rocks; the next, boulders. Suddenly the view swung about violently as Keller launched the ship into another evasive manoeuvre. They ducked and dived through space in a random, chaotic series of movements.

'Warning! Defensive failure in five clicks.'

'Almost there,' muttered Keller.

'Four clicks . . . Three . . . Two . . .'

And then they were in the asteroid field.

Giant, jagged stone walls reared up and around them on all sides. Floating mountains of rock danced across the view-screen.

'They've stopped,' called out Dray, studying the rear-view scanners. 'Even Sudor's not stupid enough to bring a battleship after us.'

'Yeah, well, let's not break out the cake and fireworks just yet,' said Keller grimly, all his attention on the forward scanners as they plunged deeper into the asteroid field. 'Getting in here is one thing, but I'd like to make it out too.'

As he spoke, two giant asteroids spun into view directly in front of them, on a collision course. Keller dived between the pair of titans, zooming through the closing gap between them a split click before they crashed together, shards of shrapnel peppering the ship's already tattered hull.

Ayl gulped. Suddenly, the blend of excitement and fear running through his veins had shifted decisively towards the latter. He bit down on his lower lip as the Trade Prince jinked in and out of gaps and around obstacles, using the main engines, thrusters and delicate manoeuvring jets to trace a path through the spinning space rocks. Several times smaller asteroids scratched the hull, knocking the ship off course. Each time, Keller just shook his head quickly and redoubled his efforts. Ayl had rarely sensed such total concentration, even among his fellow Aquanths.

Finally, though, the asteroids began to thin out. A few moments later, Keller brought the ship to a stop just beyond the far edge of the field.

'Now *that* was a rush,' he said in a half-whisper.

'We've lost contact with the battleship,' said Dray. 'Their nearest safe path through the asteroid field is at least two hours away.' She looked up from her console and grinned. 'We made it.'

'Keller,' said Ayl. There was a strange sensation in the pit of his stomach that made him think he didn't like adrenaline after all. 'Thank you.'

'Yes,' added Dray slowly. 'You have just out-flown the Bellori flagship. That was . . . impressive.'

'Uh, forget about it,' said Keller. He looked exhausted. 'What now?'

'If the Bellori will not listen, we must warn the other planets,' said Ayl.

Dray consulted her console. 'Communications are down again,' she reported. 'Destroyed by the lasers. We'll have to find an inhabited outpost and use their coms network. According to this chart, the closest is Terrial One.'

'That's a Cantorian trading post,' said Keller. 'It's hardly more than an hour from here.

Ayl nodded. 'Then let us go and see your people.'

10

The three of them sat in silence for the rest of the short journey. Letting the ship take over the flying, Keller sat back and tried to relax, but he was too keyed up. Although he'd done his best to hide it, navigating through the asteroids had terrified him. A few hours ago, life had been so simple. All he'd had to worry about was which girls to flirt with, which parties to go to, and how to persuade his father to buy him the latest racer. He'd certainly never had to fight for his life. The others didn't seem to realize how close they'd come to death in the asteroid field. One false move, and they would all have been smashed to atoms.

But, said a tiny voice inside his head, *we weren't. Thanks to me*.

It felt strange to think that he had saved two other lives as well as his own. Once this was all over – as it would be very soon – he'd have some impressive stories to tell.

'Approaching Terrial One,' said the ship.

'Oh,' breathed Ayl, his eyes bright. 'It's *huge*!'

The shining carbotanium bulk of the space station grew until it filled the whole view-screen. Terrial One was the largest orbital trading platform Cantor owned. A huge spherical city floating in space, run by a Trade Council of leading Cantorians, it acted as clearing house for the hundreds of species that came to the Trinity System to trade. Most of the platform was given over to docking facilities and warehousing – huge holding bays stacked full with the produce of countless worlds – but the soul of the place was the souk, the giant central market where the traders mixed and anything could be bought or sold. This, and places like it, were the source of Cantor's wealth.

As the ship glided smoothly into a private docking bay, Keller felt as if he could suddenly breathe again. Against all the odds, they had arrived safely.

'I need you two to wait here,' he said. 'I'm going straight to the Trade Council.'

'Stay here?' replied Dray. 'No. I am a Bellori warrior. I am coming to represent my people.'

'Yeah, well, at this precise moment, you don't look much like a Bellori to me,' said Keller. 'If you march in there without your armour and claim to be Iccus's daughter, we'll have a lot of explaining to do. Explaining we don't have time for.' Dray's eyes narrowed, but Keller went on. 'You're on my turf now, boss, so we play by my rules. The council will listen to me, but we can't afford to distract them.'

'Very well,' said Dray grudgingly.

'Ayl?'

'I will await your return,' said the blue-skinned boy, bowing his head slightly.

'Good,' said Keller. 'I'll make sure that the council contacts Aquanthis and Bellus as well as Cantor, and I'll be back as soon as I have news.'

Turning on his heel, he hurried to the airlock before Dray could come up with any more objections. The girl might be useful in a fight, but he really didn't need her kicking up a stink in front of the council.

Outside the ship, an egg-shaped glass transit pod was waiting on the deck. Keller settled into the plush leather seat.

'Take me to the council chamber.'

With a low hum, the pod glided across the hangar and into an access tube, then shot upwards at high speed. As the pod climbed, Keller scratched his chin thoughtfully. Ever since Dray had mentioned Terrial One, he'd been trying to remember why the name seemed significant. Unlike his father, who knew the name and position of every trader in the system, the finer details of the Cantorian trade network had never been something that interested Keller. But he knew *something* about this place. What was it . . . ?

'Council chamber,' said the pod, in the same neutral voice as the ship.

Oh well, he'd find out soon enough.

Keller stepped out into a large, elegantly furnished room decorated with exquisite crystal sculptures. A tall woman rose from behind a control desk and smiled.

'May I help you, young man?'

Keller felt his hackles rise at the patronizing tone. 'Yes, you may inform the council that Trade Prince Keller is here to see them. On a matter of grave importance.'

The woman's smile faltered. 'Of course, er, Your Highness. The council is in session at this moment. I will inform the president of your arrival. Please wait here.'

She hurried over to the large gold-studded ygdras-oak doors and put her eye to the retina scanner. After a moment, the doors opened slightly and the woman slipped through. Keller settled on to a black floating chair and waited.

And waited.

After five minutes, he started tapping his foot impatiently. What could possibly be the delay? After another couple of minutes, Keller got to his feet. This was ridiculous. He was the son of the trade king, carrying an urgent message. He shouldn't have to wait like this. He crossed to the doors and put his own eye to the scanner.

The doors did not open.

Feeling his temper rising, Keller walked right up to the doors and started pushing the great wooden barriers until they started swinging slowly inwards. They were heavy and he had to strain hard, beads of sweat appearing on his forehead and running down his back. He pushed until they were a pace apart and then looked up.

Before him was a raised semi-circular table, behind which seven white-haired men and women sat staring at him. They were all dressed in the finest clothes – silks and garuli-cottons. Jewellery sparkled on their fingers and necks. The room was just as richly decorated, with exotic wall hangings and portraits and busts of famous merchants from Cantor's past.

But Keller wasn't looking at any of this. His eyes were fixed on the figure at the centre of the table, his heart sinking as he suddenly remembered why the name Terrial One was familiar to him.

It wasn't the outpost itself he knew, it was the man who owned it.

'Ah, Trade Prince Keller,' said Tyrus smoothly. 'Sorry to have kept you.'

Ayl took a deep breath, seeking his centre. The last few hours had exposed him to emotions he had rarely experienced – certainly never this intensely. Now, more than ever before, he needed all the serenity the teachings of Aquanthis could give. The only problem was that he couldn't concentrate, not with Dray pacing back and forth like a caged animal.

He opened his eyes and looked at her. 'Would you like to meditate with me?' he asked.

'Meditate?' the Bellori snorted in response. 'I can't just sit and do nothing.'

For a moment, Ayl considered trying to explain to her that meditation was more than that, and then thought better of the idea.

'Keller told us to wait here,' he said simply. 'There is nothing else *to* do.'

'I don't take orders from a Cantorian,' Dray shot back. She started striding towards the door.

'I'm going out.'

'Wait—'

But she was gone. Ayl could hear her footsteps clanking through the corridor and out of the airlock. Then there was silence. What could he do? She was beyond reason and he certainly didn't want to stand in her way.

And anyway, now he had a chance to concentrate.

Settling into a comfortable cross-legged position, Ayl focused his mind on his breathing and his heartbeat, slowing them, calming himself. The real world seemed to fade away around him until he felt his mind floating free, his consciousness in its purest form. What he was about to try was difficult. He had only managed it once before, and then with his mother guiding him, but there was no other choice.

Picturing his mind as a glowing ball of white energy, Ayl slowly spread a finger of pure thought across the void of space, reaching back towards the conference centre where the aliens had attacked. His whole being felt like an insubstantial ribbon, stretching and contracting as it moved through the psychic ether.

In his mind's eye, Ayl could see the asteroid where his mother was, but surrounding the giant rock was a barrier through which his mind could not pass. He felt tentatively around the barrier, finding no entrance to what he knew must be inside. He tried to force his way through, but it was too strong. He might as well have been trying to dig through solid rock with his bare hands.

Ayl felt himself weakening. His mother could maintain a psychic projection for many minutes, but he was not as strong as she was. He was just about to draw back into his own body when suddenly he saw a faint light glimmering in the darkness.

Ayl was scared for an instant, but then he saw that it was another psychic projection – one with the familiar resonance of Aquanthis. A consciousness from home was exploring here as well! A moment later, the light sharpened, racing through space towards him.

As the light touched his own, Ayl felt a strange sensation, like he was one of two liquids merging together. Then, suddenly, he was flying through the galaxy faster than the speed of light, pulled along by the other mind, until finally they came to rest in a shimmering blue place.

Ayl felt his heart skip a beat. He was standing inside the atrium of the Great Temple on Aquanthis. He could feel the kiss of cool water on his skin as he stared up at the high arches, surrounded by hundreds of priests from every chapel on the planet. And before them all stood the figure of the Naptarch, his mother's closest advisor.

The ancient, wrinkled man looked at Ayl with relief, and his voice slipped into Ayl's mind. *We thought you lost. You and your mother.*

I escaped, he thought back. *Let me show you . . .*

Ayl concentrated hard on his memories of the attack. He showed the assembled priests the aliens – the way they moved and how they had invaded his thoughts. He showed them Keller and Dray, although he was careful not to show them Dray without her armour. The young warrior had saved his life; he would not betray her secret. He showed them their escape from the asteroid, their encounter with the Bellori and their arrival at Terrial One.

As the memories passed to the priests their very substance seemed to waver – the horror momentarily weakening their discipline. Terrible as it was to live through it again, Ayl felt overwhelmed with relief as he told his story. Now at least his people knew what they faced. Now they could decide what to do.

My mother is still on the asteroid, he finished. *But they have cut her off from my mind. Who are these creatures? What do they want? What are we going to do?*

For a moment, silence filled the waters of the temple. Then a single mind whispered a single word.

Conclave.

Ayl's heart sank. A conclave was a psychic meeting of every mind on Aquanthis: every man, woman and child coming together to make a decision. It was the epitome of democracy, something no non-psychic race could ever fully appreciate. But it took time. Every mind had to be linked, then told what had happened, then given time to consider and discuss.

But we must act now, he pleaded. *We must save my mother!*

Conclave. The thought was being taken up by other minds now, repeated again and again in a chorus of agreement.

Ayl felt frustration overwhelming him. *There's no time!*

Conclave, repeated the Naptarch. *We know your feelings, Ayl, and will consider them, but you cannot be part of this conclave. You are too far away, and not strong enough to maintain the link over so great a distance. When the conclave has reached accord, I will tell you what it has decreed.*

But—

I am sorry, Ayl. We thank you for bringing us this warning. Now we must decide. Farewell.

No, wait!

But it was too late. The image of the temple was already dissolving around him. Ayl struggled, trying to force it back into focus, but it was like trying to hold back the tide.

Slowly, as if waking from a dream, Ayl's mind floated back into his body. He blinked, staring around. He was back on board the Cantorian cruiser, solarpaces from his home and his people.

Now all he could do was wait.

Dray stomped down yet another featureless metallic corridor, letting her anger drive her feet. She was lost, and she knew it. Couldn't the Cantorians at least have put up some signs to guide their visitors? And if this was a trading post, where were all the traders?

For a moment, she thought of trying to retrace her steps. But she couldn't turn back now and lose face in front of Ayl. Besides, she might be lost but she wasn't in any danger. This was a Cantorian outpost and she was Bellori. Even without her armour, there was surely nobody here that could beat her in a fight. Anyway, this was her first trip off Bellus. And if her father got wind that she'd passed top secret security codes to a Cantorian, it would probably be her last too, so she was curious to see a little of the universe while she had the chance.

Dray glanced down at the smooth, pink skin of her arm. Normally, there was no chance a Bellori could go anywhere unnoticed. But now she was out of her armour, she looked enough like a Cantorian to pass as one of them. That could have its advantages too . . .

She came to a door and palmed the control. It slid aside and Dray was instantly bombarded with a riot of noise and colour. In front of her stretched a long, multi-storied promenade of market stalls and restaurants. She could see countless incredible objects for sale: crimson glow-lamps that seemed to float in the air, musical instruments that played themselves, animals of all shapes and sizes in cages and on leads. But the most incredible sight was the mass of aliens thronging the walkways. A few paces away, a pair of green-scaled Ledoptrians were bartering with a spider-shaped robot; above their heads flapped what looked like a giant bird with vivid orange wings; a gaggle of masked, knee-high aliens scurried past, dragging sacks of golden grain; and among them all were the Cantorians, haggling, bartering and laughing.

Without realizing she was moving, Dray stepped through the doorway and followed her sense of smell towards a fruit-seller's stall. Big floating containers were overflowing with spiky purple balls the size of her fist. They smelt like nothing she had ever known before, sweet and spicy. She picked one up and held it to her nose, breathing the scent in deeply.

'Wise choice, my lady,' said a fat man who appeared beside her. 'Fresh from the forests of Al-Bara this very morning. You won't find finer anywhere in the souk.'

'What are they?' said Dray. She didn't trust the man, but she had to know what she was holding. To think that people ate these incredible things! The food on Bellus was all so . . . grey.

'Agaral seeds, my dear,' said the merchant. A smile stretched quickly across his face but didn't reach his eyes. 'For someone as pretty as you, I'm sure I can give a discount. Say fifty cubits for a kilo?'

'Oh, I don't have any money,' Dray replied. 'Can I try just one?'

She hadn't considered she might have to pay for something to eat. At home, everyone was assigned the same daily ration, regardless of who they were.

'Try one?' laughed the merchant, the smile disappearing from his face. 'What do you think I am, a charity? Get out of here, you little thief.' He snatched the fruit back from her and threw it into the basket.

'What did you call me?' Dray squared up to the

merchant in an instant. The man stepped back nervously, and several nearby Cantorians also turned to stare at her. She couldn't afford to risk any trouble. If people found out who she was – that the Bellori were not the race of armoured giants everyone in the galaxy believed them to be – it would be the greatest disaster in the history of her race. And it would be all her fault. Against all of her instincts, she resisted the urge to stuff the spiky fruit down the fat man's throat.

'I am *not* a thief,' she said hoarsely. She turned to the staring crowd. 'What are you looking at?'

At the sound of her growling voice, most of the onlookers suddenly decided they had somewhere else to be. In moments, the crowd had melted away, leaving just one man behind. He was taller and leaner than most Cantorians, with long, dark hair that flowed down to his shoulders. A long scar stretched over one side of his face from his forehead to his chin. For an instant, his eyes locked on to Dray's, narrowing as if she was someone he knew and didn't like. Then he turned and strode away with a long, easy gait.

Dray dug her nails into her palms angrily, forcing herself to calm down and focus. Something about the man made her uncomfortable. It was almost as if he knew she was hiding something. Whatever it was, one thing was clear: she was attracting attention. She should have stayed on the ship like Keller had wanted. No matter how curious she was, this was no place for her.

She turned and walked quickly back the way she'd come, trying to find her way back to the ship. But she must have wandered further into the souk than she realized. She couldn't see the door – or any other exits for that matter.

Pushing her way through the crowds, Dray felt her lungs tighten with fear. What if she couldn't find her way back? Would the others leave without her? She *had* to get out. She looked around wildly for any clue to which way she should go.

And froze.

Standing in the aisle a few paces ahead, his dark eyes fixed on her, was the strange, scar-faced man.

Turning on her heel, Dray dived back into the throng. But now she could sense more eyes on her. A different man was walking fast along the aisle to her right, level with her. She doubled her pace, almost knocking over an elderly Cantorian woman, who waved an ivory-tipped walking stick angrily as Dray elbowed her way on.

'Out of my way!' she barked. 'Coming through!'

Glancing over her shoulder, Dray saw that the first

man was following her too, but he was being slowed up by the crowds. If she was quick, she might be able to lose both her pursuers.

Without pausing to think, Dray dropped to the floor and rolled left, under a hover-stall selling ornamental weapons. She felt the odd tingle of anti-grav against her skin for a moment, then she was up again. Snatching a jewelled dagger from the stall, she dropped and rolled a second time. Feet pounded the ground beside her head and she had to snatch away her fingers to avoid being trampled, but she made it through to the next aisle.

There were fewer people here, and it was easier to move. Breaking into a jog, Dray hurried down the aisle, looking left and right. There was no sign of either of her pursuers. Running her tongue over her dry lips, she stopped outside an empty shop to get her bearings and her breath back. Mission accomplished.

Suddenly she felt a hard, cracking blow to the back of her head. She tried to cry out, but her voice didn't seem to work and her knees buckled. Hands reached out and grabbed her, dragging her roughly backwards as the world faded to darkness.

11

'Tyrus,' said Keller, trying his best to hide his surprise. 'Why have I been kept waiting?'

'I hadn't realized you were trying to get in, My Liege,' said Tyrus, a sly smile creeping across his face. 'Perhaps the door mechanism is broken. But what an impressive display of strength you gave us. That door has always been obstinate.'

'Remember who you're talking to, Tyrus,' snapped Keller. 'You shouldn't play games with a prince.'

'Not even a prince who so loves to play games with his father's subjects?' Tyrus replied, his voice suddenly cold. Before Keller could reply, Tyrus waved a hand dismissively. 'But what is it you want? Please be brief. Some of us actually *work* for a living around here.'

Keller felt his face flush as several of the other councillors laughed at their leader's jibe.

'The asteroid conference has been attacked,' he said. He looked straight at Tyrus as he spoke, putting as much authority into his voice as he could muster. He thought back to all the times he had heard his father speak, and tried to find the same rhythm. 'Aliens have taken the trade king captive, along with General Iccus of Bellus and the High Priestess of Aquanthis. Only I and the heirs to the two other worlds escaped. We very nearly didn't. There is a horde of deadly creatures on that asteroid, ready to tear their way into the heart of the Trinity System. You must send a message to the three worlds to warn them. The lives of everyone on those planets could be at stake.'

Tyrus stared back at Keller, his eyes wide.

Yes, that shut you up, didn't it, you old goat? thought Keller darkly.

Tyrus tugged thoughtfully on his beard. 'Aliens, hmm?' he mused. 'What kind of aliens?'

'Some kind of giant insect,' said Keller, spreading his arms to give an impression of size. 'Bigger than a man and armed with vicious claws. I've never seen anything like them.'

'And where did they come from?' asked Tyrus, leaning forward.

'I'm not sure,' Keller replied, shaking his head. 'But they can survive in space. Maybe they came in that way. They took us completely by surprise.'

'And how many did you say there were?'

'I don't know exactly,' Keller answered impatiently. Surely even a blockhead like Tyrus could see that these details didn't matter as much as getting out the warning? 'We were chased by hundreds, and each one could rip apart a Cantorian without even thinking about it. We must warn the planets now!'

'All in good time,' said Tyrus, sitting back and blinking. 'Now, let me see if I understand correctly. An army of giant alien insects has attacked the summit conference. They were so *deadly* that they overpowered not only your father's bodyguard, but also an elite squad of Bellori, the most highly-trained and effective military force in known space. Then, despite demonstrating such incredible martial prowess, they somehow let a spoiled teenager and two other pampered heirs escape their clutches. You then came here – heroically, may I add? – you then *heroically* came here, to warn everyone and become the saviour of the Trinity System. Is that about right?'

'More or less—' began Keller, but Tyrus cut him off with a wave of his hand.

'Can I ask just one more question?' said the old man, rising slowly to his feet. '*Do you think you can make a fool of me again?*' he roared.

'I'm not trying to make a fool of anyone,' Keller shouted. 'You've got to believe me – what I'm telling you is true!'

'Fellow members of the Trade Council,' said Tyrus, speaking as if Keller wasn't even in the room. 'I move for a vote to dismiss this nonsense immediately. This boy is a known trickster and charlatan. All in favour?'

'Aye,' chorused the other six councillors.

'Motion passed,' said Tyrus, staring down at Keller with a smile of triumph. 'You are dismissed, Your Highness.'

A stinging slap across the face brought Dray to her senses.

Before she could focus her eyes, she was dragged up from the ground into a kneeling position. Her wrists had been bound behind her back, causing her shoulders to ache, but that was nothing compared to the pounding between her ears. Someone grabbed her roughly by the chin.

'Time to wake,' they hissed.

She was in a dark room, dusty with age and disuse, surrounded by half a dozen Cantorians. She fixed her eyes on the man who held her, a thick-necked, strong-armed brute.

'Strike me again and I will kill you,' she said, and spat in his face.

Her attacker made a noise that might have been a grunt of approval. Then he asked, 'Who are you?'

'Who are *you*?' replied Dray. 'Tell me your name and I'll make you a grave marker, Cantorian.'

The man raised his fist.

'Enough.'

A tall figure stepped out from behind Dray. Even in the dim light, she recognized him immediately. The scar-faced man from the souk.

'You forget yourself, Gort. We have sworn never again to use violence needlessly, remember?'

Gort lowered his head and the man from the souk turned to face Dray, dropping into an easy crouch in front of her. 'We are no more Cantorian than you are – as you know very well. How did you find us?'

'Find you?' she said, grimacing. 'I don't even know you.'

'Don't lie to me.'

'I am not a liar,' growled Dray. 'Cut me loose and I'll show you what I am.'

'I already know what you are,' snapped the tall man. 'And I have killed better warriors than you many times.'

Dray eyed him warily. He talked like a warrior. He

even *moved* like a warrior, she now realized – the casual way he had carried himself in the souk when she had first seen him was the confidence of a fighting man. But the Cantorians had no army. So how could this man be a warrior? Unless . . .

'Yes,' said the man softly. 'I am from *Bellus*.' He spat the word like a curse.

Dray shook her head. 'From Bellus?' she whispered, her anger replaced with amazement. 'But where is your armour?'

The man stared into her eyes and spoke with a quiet intensity. 'My name is Tudeno. I was born on Bellus, but I am no longer Bellori. I was once a warrior. I fought and killed until I knew nothing but blood. I was a monster. I took off my armour when I saw that my children deserved a better life. These few agreed with me. We banded together, stole a ship and fled with our families. We wandered for many cycles, but in the end we arrived here, where no one knew who we truly were. Where we are no longer monsters.'

Dray couldn't believe what Tudeno was saying. She had never heard of a Bellori soldier ever choosing to live without their armour. It was impossible! And yet, here one was, looking her straight in the eyes, daring her to call him a liar.

'And now, after all these turns, Iccus has sent you here to find us. To bring our families back under his control.' Tudeno stood up. 'We will not go.'

Dray raised her head. 'You have to listen to me. I have never heard of you before. I don't care who you are or what you've done. There are more important things than dealing with deserters now.'

As she spoke, she remembered her last exchange with Sudor. She had refused to follow his orders, run away from him rather than submit to his commands. Did that make her a deserter too? No, what she had done, she had done for the good of Bellus, even if Sudor couldn't see it. And she could do more, with the help of these people. Whatever else they were, they were still trained fighters. If Sudor wouldn't join her, perhaps they would. But only if they knew what they were fighting for.

Struggling to her feet, she looked at each of the exiles in turn. 'I am Dray, daughter of General Iccus.' A murmur of dismay passed around the room. 'You may think that I am your enemy, but I'm not. In fact, I need your help. There is a new threat to all the peoples of the Trinity System. An alien force, already here, preparing to attack the planets. Deadly insects, larger and stronger than any man. And there are thousands, perhaps millions of them.'

'She's lying, trying to save herself,' growled the man who'd slapped her.

'Call me a liar again and I will rip out your heart,' snapped Dray. The warrior stepped forward, ready to strike her, but Tudeno put up his hand.

'She is Bellori,' he said quietly. 'I believe her.' He nodded to the general's daughter and the room was quiet again, everyone waiting for her to continue.

'If these creatures get off the asteroid,' she went on, 'no one is safe. Bellori, Cantorians, Aquanths – we'll all suffer. My people won't help me. Sudor thinks I'm a traitor. I need troops to go back to the asteroid with me. You were Bellori warriors once. Even without your armour, you are the best fighters in the galaxy. Please, won't you join me?'

Tudeno looked at her, weighing her words, his eyes narrowed to slits. Dray held her breath. Even though these Bellori had abandoned the military chain of command, it was clear he was their leader. The others would follow him in whatever he chose.

For a long moment, Tudeno stood motionless. Then, slowly, he reached behind him and drew out a long, serrated blade from a hidden sheath. Its edges were dented and chipped from use, but Dray could see it had been kept razor-sharp. As Tudeno stepped towards her, she forced herself not to flinch. If this man wanted to kill her, she was powerless to stop him.

Tudeno stared at the blade for a moment, then reached around Dray and cut her bonds.

'You are a brave warrior,' he said slowly. 'And I believe that yours is a battle worth fighting.'

Dray's heart leapt.

'But we cannot help you. We took an oath. We can't break it now, and return to the way of life we fled from.'

'You will have to fight these aliens,' said Dray, resisting the urge to rub her sore wrists. 'If not now, then later.'

Tudeno shook his head. 'I'm sorry. But you are free to go. And good luck.'

Dray pushed roughly past him. At the door, she looked back at the exiles, disappointment bubbling up inside her.

'You are traitors and cowards,' she hissed, unable to conceal her scorn. None of the men could meet her eyes.

She turned on her heel and walked away.

Ayl sat alone in the main compartment of the ship. His eyes were open but unfocused as he practised the discipline of *Joh-Il-Noor* – the ordering of the self. One by one, he brought to mind all the events that had happened since the attack on the asteroid, assessing his thoughts and deeds.

He was not impressed. He had acted rashly. He had made snap judgements. He had been pleased by the death of the alien creatures. He had even attempted to mind-share with an outsider. By the standards of his people, he had failed.

But Ayl didn't feel like a failure. He had acted to preserve life. He had escaped to warn others of the horror that had arrived. He had even begun to understand his Cantorian and Bellori companions. They didn't seem to be the lower life-forms he had been raised to believe they were. Even though they had flaws, they were every bit as intelligent as Aquanths.

Ayl . . . Ayl . . .

A musical voice pierced his thoughts. The Naptarch! Ayl felt his chest swell with hope. The conclave must have finished sooner than he had expected. Closing his eyes, he felt his consciousness being pulled back to the Great Temple. The atrium was empty this time, save for the solitary figure of the Naptarch.

The conclave is over and we have decreed how to defend Aquanthis.

We will fight the aliens?

The Naptarch shook his head, his face so full of pity that Ayl knew that there was no good news.

We will hide. The world-ocean must be kept safe. We will activate the Shroud.

Ayl blinked. The Shroud was a legendary psychic cloak that could cover the whole of Aquanthis, making it invisible to anyone outside the planet's atmosphere. Impossible to locate and contact, even to those with psychic powers.

But what about my mother, Ayl pleaded. *What about me?*

The Naptarch bowed his head. I am sorry. *The high priestess is beyond our reach, and you are too far from home. We cannot wait for you. The risk is too great.*

Ayl clenched his fist, digging his nails into his palms. He had to keep control. He had to convince them not to hide. But a storm of emotion leaked out of him.

You are abandoning me and my mother! You are abandoning everyone on Bellus and Cantor!

I am sorry, repeated the Naptarch, stepping back in shock. *Good luck, Ayl.*

'No!' Ayl screamed. 'You can't do this!'

But even as he cried out, Ayl suddenly found himself back on board the tiny Cantorian ship. Anger lending him focus, he sent out his mind again, stretching across the abyss of space towards his home. But there was nothing there. His planet was gone. He couldn't even sense a barrier like the one the aliens had somehow created around the asteroid. It was as though Aquanthis had never existed.

Ayl drew a shuddering breath. First his mother had been taken from him, and now his whole planet. He had never felt so alone. Desperation swamping him, he widened his search, sending out uncontrolled flashes of psychic energy, desperately feeling for another mind – any mind.

Then he felt it. A faint touch, little more than a brush against his mind, but familiar. Was it Dray? Or maybe Keller? Ayl stood up quickly, wiping his eyes. He couldn't let them see him like this; the embarrassment would be too much.

But as he struggled to compose himself, Ayl realized that the consciousness wasn't either of his companions. The emotions were too crude and basic. And although the sensation was faint, it was close. Very close.

Blinking away the last tears, Ayl glanced around the compartment. There was no one else there. Only the body of the alien, bundled into a corner, a collection of scorched insect parts. Tentatively, Ayl probed it gently with his mind. Surely it couldn't be . . .

'Agh!' Even though he was paces away from the creature, Ayl leapt backwards, his spine slamming against the wall. The touch against his mind had been faint, perhaps even fainter than the first. But there was no doubt that it was there, and no doubt where it was coming from.

The alien's mouth opened slowly. Forgetting his disgust, the Aquanth stepped carefully towards it. He leaned forward. *It's dead*, he thought. *It must be.*

A jagged limb shot out from the mass of body parts and knocked him off his feet. He hit his head hard on the ground and his vision went blurry. A large shape jerked towards him. He blinked and his eyes cleared.

The nightmare creature was crawling in his direction, fanged mandibles snapping. Ready to kill.

12

Dray was deep in thought about Tudeno as she walked through the bare metal corridor back to the ship. A Bellori warrior, a strong one too if she was any judge, renouncing violence. Not just that, but leading a sizable group of soldiers away with him. It was unheard of. It was treasonous. Not to do your duty, for whatever reason, was shameful.

But then she thought about all the times she'd wanted to escape, to get away from her father. She shook her head. She'd wanted to be normal, to be a warrior and fight in the army. Not to hide on some Cantorian outpost. She rubbed her jaw, feeling the bruises where she'd been beaten. When this was all over she'd come back and find the mullock who'd hit her. She'd find out how tough he was when she wasn't tied up.

She rounded the corner into the hangar and looked up at the battered hulk of the ship that had brought her here. There was nothing to do now but wait for Keller, leaving her fate in the hands of a trader . . .

There was a bright flash of light through the craft's open hatchway. A moment later came the *whoomp* of a k-gun blast and the chiming of shattered glass. Her instincts kicked in. She bounded up the access ramp in two long strides, leaping through the door – ready for anything. A manic scrabbling was coming from the forward compartment and she dashed towards it. As she passed through the door a light flashed and she heard the *whoomp* again. A chair exploded in front of her and the air in the cabin filled with strips of leather and foam padding.

She dived to the side, catching a glimpse of Ayl wrestling with her weapon. He was desperately trying to aim the weapon as he crawled backwards, away from . . .

'Ayl!' she yelled. 'What the—'

A serrated, spear-like limb arced through the air at her. She twisted her body just in time to avoid it, catching sight of the injured alien. It was frantically dragging itself towards her, waving one leg about and beating its other damaged ones on the ground.

Ayl let off another shot, hitting a wall panel and sending sparks everywhere. 'I can't hit it!' cried the boy. 'I can't hit it!'

The creature's leg swung through the air again, this time at her head. She dodged and grabbed the limb with both hands, pulling the beast towards her as she lashed out with a boot. The contact jarred her whole body. It was like kicking a ferro-concrete wall. The alien jerked back its arm and sent Dray crashing into a wall. She slumped to the ground, the breath driven out of her by the impact, and looked up. The monster was right before her, its deadly leg raised to deliver the killing blow. But standing just behind it was Ayl, with the k-gun shakily pointed towards them both.

Ayl felt his legs tremble as he tried to aim the unfamiliar weapon. The alien lurched towards Dray, its leg sweeping down to stab into her. *Pull the trigger*, he thought. *Pull the trigger!*

Then, suddenly, looking down the barrel at the monster, the world froze. Time seemed to stop as smoke hung motionless in the air. Without thinking, Ayl's psychic sense reached out and he felt the insect's mind, like a bright flame. It burnt with a murderous rage, a vicious desperation. He traced its edges and probed inside it, unable to stop himself. It was driven by a primordial, animal instinct to survive, but that instinct came from somewhere else. But where . . .

A connection. The slightest gossamer thread stretching from the alien's mind through space. Impossibly thin but incredibly strong, pulsing with life. *Fascinating*, he thought. Nothing he had ever seen even came close to this, and he'd never read about it in the temple library. It was more than just a mental connection. It was as though the creature's mind was a tiny part of something larger, as if the creature was nothing more than a sucker on a tentacle. But what was it attached to? He had to know. Ayl forced his mind to stretch out like a ribbon again, and followed the thread.

It led him through space, twisting and turning, pulsing and vibrating. A few times he almost lost it. Like spider's silk, it disappeared when seen from the wrong angle. But he always found it again, knowing where it would lead him. Back to the asteroid. Back to where all this began. This time he struck the alien barrier, coming up against it hard, butting against it in his excitement. He knew there was a way in. He imagined grasping the thread, pulling himself along, hand over hand. It led to a microscopic dent in the blockade, too small even for atoms. Squeezing and straining, he pushed through the hole until, at last, he was in!

Rather than the asteroid's rock and metal he saw hundreds and thousands more threads, each with a bright light at the end. There were so many it looked like a field of golden Cantorian wheat, swaying in a breeze. But it wasn't flat, it was spherical, each of the threads leading towards a roaring fire at the centre.

He dived closer and a wave of violent emotions burst over him, almost washing him away. It suddenly struck him that at the end of each of those glowing threads was one of the aliens. There must be thousands, all of them connected to a single mind. A single evil presence directing thousands of murderous aliens.

Scared of getting lost in the horde, Ayl kept close to the first thread, the one that could lead him back to the ship. He refused to turn back though: he was here to find his mother. He travelled on, getting closer to the presence at the centre. The controlling mind burnt brilliantly now. Like a fierce star, it blotted out the other sources of light. But there, just beside it, were three coloured lights – one green, one red and one, ever so slightly brighter, blue.

Mother! he called. *Mother!*

Suddenly, the central mind turned to look at Ayl. The full force of its light burnt into his mind and he felt as though he was on fire. He grabbed the thread and began to pull himself away as fast as he could but the presence screamed at him. Its voice was like the weight of an ocean crashing down on him, piercing him and shaking him until he thought he would go mad.

We are the Nara-Karith! You will die! It shot a giant ball of flame along the thread Ayl was holding. When the fire reached him, agony spread through his entire being. It dragged him along with incredible speed. He tried to let go, to escape from the pain, but it held on to him. He was propelled back into the shuttle, back into the flight cabin, and back into his own body.

His eyes flicked open to see the alien spin away from Dray and face him. It hissed and its whole body trembled with rage. It leapt through the air at him.

He pulled the trigger.

Keller ran into the cabin in time to see the alien burst apart in mid-air. The Aquanth dropped the gun and fell to his knees, sobbing. Dray's front was splattered with a thick slime and she was looking at what was left of the alien carcass on the floor in front of her. The room was trashed. Panels were hanging loose and screens were shattered, glass shards spread across the ground. The couches were pulverized and one of the ceiling lights was flickering.

Ayl started rocking back and forth on the ground, hugging his knees and mumbling to himself. The trade prince went over and crouched by him, but looked at Dray.

'What happened in here?' he asked her. She was trying to clean off the slime with a scrap of leather. *Not slime. Alien blood*, he thought.

'I don't know,' she said, sounding shocked herself. 'It could have killed me, but it turned on him instead.'

'It was alive,' whispered Ayl. His eyes were wide as he locked gazes with the trade prince. Keller put a hand on the other boy's shoulder and tried to smile.

'It's over now—' he started, but the Aquanth pushed his hand away.

'It was alive!' he yelled, surprising Keller, who stood up and took a step back. 'It was alive and I've killed it! By The Divine, what have I done?'

Dray knelt down and looked the blue-skinned boy in the eyes. 'You did what was necessary,' she said, slowly and quietly. 'You saved my life.'

'I saw its mind,' Ayl whispered, almost to himself. 'I never imagined . . . It was *evil*.'

'You saw its mind?' asked Keller. 'I don't understand.'

'My people . . .' said the Aquanth, trying to control his sobs. 'You would call us telepathic.'

'Telepathic? But that's—' began Dray.

'Impossible,' finished Keller.

'It's true,' said Ayl.

'No way,' said the trade prince. 'Not outside of stories, anyway.'

'The High Command has been experimenting with mental communication for many turns,' said the Bellori, 'so we can give military commands telepathically. But we never got anywhere, so how can you expect me to believe—'

'We've been attacked by aliens,' interrupted the Aquanth. 'We've outrun a Bellori battleship. We've seen beneath your armour, Dray. Is it so hard to believe my people have secrets too?'

'When you put it like that . . .' said the trade prince. 'But it's so weird.'

'It's not weird to Aquanths,' said Ayl. 'It is all we know. Our minds are always joined, we always know what each other are feeling. It is unnatural to be alone in your thoughts, like I am now, completely cut off from my people.'

'Well, if it's any consolation, we're all cut off from our people now,' said Dray.

'You can read my mind, if it makes you feel better,' suggested Keller, keen to put Ayl's skills to the test.

'Thanks, but I'll pass,' Ayl said with a weak smile. 'Anyway, Aquanths aren't the only ones who read minds – the aliens are telepathic too. They call themselves the Nara-Karith. There's one in control of them all, like a queen commanding a hive. But all it wants is to kill.'

'There's only one mind between them?' asked Dray.

'Yes. No.' Ayl looked confused for a moment. 'It's complicated. There's one intelligent one, the one in control, who holds everything together. The rest are like animals.'

'We need to get to your planet,' said the girl. 'Your people can help us.'

'They won't help,' Ayl said, not meeting either of their eyes. 'They're too scared. They've hidden our world to protect it.'

'They can hide a world?' said the Cantorian, whistling through his teeth and looking at Dray. 'That's actually . . . really cool.'

'I don't suppose the Cantorians have any secrets?' asked the Bellori.

'What you see is what you get with us,' Keller said, smiling proudly at the other two.

'That's because what you see is a conniving, self-seeking, profit-motivated swindler,' said Dray. She stared at Keller for a moment before breaking into a big grin.

'No way! Was that a joke?' the trade prince started laughing and slapped the Aquanth's back. 'The Bellori told a joke, Ayl! Not a great one, but we can work on that later, I guess.' The other boy laughed too, but quickly became serious again.

'When my mind was at the asteroid, I saw the alien's plans,' Ayl said, looking at each of his companions in turn. 'It is going to attack the three worlds with overwhelming force. Did you get the warning out?' Ayl asked Keller.

The Cantorian felt his heart sink. 'No,' the trade prince admitted through gritted teeth. 'They didn't believe me.' He told them about his reputation and about Tyrus, hating every moment of it. He felt his face go red, embarrassed to tell these two what people thought of him. But stronger than his shame was his anger at the old mullock that had ridiculed him. If that has-been didn't have the sense to know what was good for him, then Keller would just have to do without him.

'There's no choice now,' he said to Dray and Ayl.

'This is a war. Aquanthis has disappeared. Cantor won't listen. There's only one people who can save us – we're going to Bellus.'

13

Dray saw the Aquanth's eyes go wide in surprise.

'Is that such a good idea,' said Ayl, 'after what happened with Sudor?'

'Sudor is a politician,' said Dray, savouring the chance to insult her rival. She could feel the muscles in her shoulders tense as she thought about General Iccus's favourite. 'He's taken over in my father's absence, but that doesn't mean he controls all Bellori. If I can talk to the High Command, I might be able to convince them to attack.'

'Convince a Bellori to attack?' said Keller, grinning again. 'Shouldn't be too difficult . . .'

Dray rolled her eyes, refusing to let the Cantorian's joke get a rise out of her. She knew he didn't mean any harm – his teasing was good-natured, unlike Sudor's jibes. Anyway, she needed to save all her energy for the battles that lay ahead.

'I'm sorry,' said the Aquanth, 'but I still don't

understand. Are we simply going to fly to Bellus and ask for help? What makes you think they're going to listen this time?'

Dray didn't answer. She found a cloth and did her best to wipe the alien blood off her clothing.

'Yuck,' she said, scrubbing at the yellow slime. 'This stuff is disgusting.'

When she'd cleaned herself off, Dray knelt down and picked up the k-gun that Ayl had dropped. She turned the rifle over in her hands and checked the charge. She started unclipping sections carefully but at speed, stripping the weapon down into its component parts, setting a few aside for cleaning. She'd done the same kind of thing hundreds of times; it always cleared her mind.

'What are you doing?' asked Keller.

'Thinking,' she replied. She wiped insect blood from the parts with a leather rag from one of the chairs. She then clipped the parts back together and looked at the heavy rifle in her hands. It didn't have much range, and it wasn't particularly accurate. But the k-gun had always been her favourite weapon during training sessions back home. Up close, there was nothing more devastating. She smiled to herself as she racked the pump-action mechanism under the barrel.

'Careful where you point that thing,' said the Cantorian. 'Listen, Ayl's got a point. Sudor's probably got the whole planet on the lookout for you. And I don't fancy trying to out-fly any more battleships.' He waved his hand to indicate the damaged cabin. 'I'm not convinced the ship will get out of dock anyway. We need you to get us in.'

'I have an idea,' she said.

As they followed Dray through the bare metal corridors to the souk, Ayl could feel Keller's eyes on him. The Cantorian had been looking at him strangely since they left the ship and it was making him self-conscious.

'What?' Ayl asked him.

'So . . . what am I thinking, then?' asked the trade prince.

'Nothing very interesting,' said Ayl and smiled to let him know it was a joke. As the trade prince laughed, Ayl thought about his friends back home. The quiet, serious boys he studied with were nothing like the Cantorian. Most of them rarely left the temple and certainly none of them had been off-world. He wondered what they'd think if they could see him, the star pupil, with traders and warriors, on a space station . . .

The trio walked through a doorway and suddenly Ayl was assaulted by a riot of noise and colour. He took in the sights of the souk with wide-eyed wonder, all thoughts of home forgotten. He'd never seen so many different races in one place. The spectacle made him forget their problems, if only for an instant.

'When this is over,' he said to Keller, 'I would appreciate it if you would show me the rest of Terrial One.'

'Ayl, old buddy,' said the trade prince, grinning and putting an arm round the Aquanth's shoulder. 'Terrial One is nothing. When this is over, I'll show you Cantor.'

'Quiet,' Dray snapped at them. Ayl saw that she was standing very still and staring at a tall man with a scar across his face. The adult nodded, then turned away and disappeared into the crowd. 'Stick close to me,' said the girl, as she moved to follow.

He caught sight of the man again a little further on. They were being led through the crowds and down a shabby-looking corridor. Away from all the shoppers, the space station seemed to take on a tight, claustrophobic air. The man stopped outside an abandoned shop. As the three teenagers got close, six other rough men emerged from the shadows. Ayl felt his knees start to shake. They were outnumbered and surrounded. Even Keller had gone quiet and the Aquanth could see him holding his shoulders back and sucking his stomach in, trying to look taller and fitter.

'Tudeno,' said Dray, to the scar-faced man. 'We need to talk.'

'Who are they?' he asked, gesturing at Ayl and Keller.

'They're with me,' she said. The blue-skinned boy could feel the weight of the men's gazes on him. There was something familiar, yet hostile, about their auras. After a moment, Tudeno turned and led the way into the shop. The three friends followed him into a back room, the six heavies right behind.

'I need armour for three,' she said, deadpan. 'And a Bellori shuttle.'

'Dray,' said Tudeno coldly, 'I told you before, we rejected all of that when we came here.' There was something primal about them both that fascinated Ayl, regardless of how scared he was. He looked at Tudeno with his mind's eye and realized – he was Bellori. Despite the man's hard exterior, inside he was fighting a turmoil of emotion. There was warmth and respect for Dray that the older man refused to show. But there was also a determination to protect his followers.

'This is more important than your *oath*,' she almost spat the word. The two Bellori, heir and exile, stood staring at each other for a moment. No one else spoke. Then Tudeno pulled a key-card from a shirt pocket and threw it to Dray. She snatched it out of the air and looked at it.

'Quadrant A, hangar C12,' said Tudeno. 'You'll find what you need there.' The old warrior was so pleased to help that Ayl could see the relief in his mind.

'This is your last chance,' said Dray, looking at each of the other men in turn. 'Join us now, and glory will be yours.'

'We cannot,' said Tudeno, looking at the floor.

Dray pointed at the leader of the exiles, her finger like a dagger point. There was venom in her voice when she spoke. 'Even the Aquanth and the Cantorian are braver than you. Do you understand? You are less of a warrior than a seaweed-eating priest.' She turned and stormed out.

Before he followed, Ayl took one last look at the exile. The Bellori's mind was ablaze with shame.

As he and Keller went after Dray, he turned to the Cantorian. 'What's wrong with seaweed?' he asked.

Keller couldn't help but be disappointed. When people talked about Bellori spacecraft, they always used words like 'hulking' and 'menacing'. What they found was a dented little ship in need of a paint-job. A few old particle beam weapons were attached to the hull, but they looked too rusted to work. Dray waved the key-card and an access hatch swung open with a loud, rasping creak. 'Are you sure this thing is going to fly?' he asked.

'It's Bellori,' answered the girl, sounding a little doubtful herself. 'Of course it'll fly.'

Keller gave Ayl a look of mock-terror behind Dray's back as he followed her in.

There was just room for all three of them in the forward cabin – one pilot's seat, which Dray took this time, and two weapons consoles. The controls were primitive compared to the sleek Cantorian cruiser they'd flown in earlier, but easier to understand. The trade prince took one look and knew he could fly it blindfolded.

Dray ran through the pre-flight checks quickly and they were out in space within minutes. She plotted a course then turned to face the other two. 'We'll be in orbit around Bellus in under an hour,' she said. 'It's time we were properly dressed.'

'Dressed? Are you going to put us in uniform, then?' asked Keller. The Bellori looked at him and smiled, which just made him nervous.

'Come on,' she said, and led them both to the rear compartment. The small box of a room had shutters pulled down along three of the walls. Dray hit a switch and the shutters rolled up, revealing three suits of armour standing in recesses. The suits were empty, looking like someone had taken a giant tin opener to them, and Keller could see the sophisticated machinery on the inside.

'Awesome,' whispered the Cantorian. 'You mean, we get to wear Bellori armour?'

'We're going to High Command,' replied the girl. 'The single most heavily guarded facility in known space. How else did you think we'd be able to sneak in?'

'Like I said,' answered Keller. 'Awesome.' There was a mature, sensible part of his mind that told him it was the most rational option, the only way past Bellori border control. But there was a much louder, more energetic part of his mind that just wanted to stomp about and pretend to be General Iccus.

'Ayl,' said the Bellori. 'You're first.' She led the Aquanth over to one of the suits and made him step backwards into it slowly. She held his hands as he got his feet into the boots and then made sure he was strapped in tightly. 'Now just press your head back . . .' Ayl did as he was told and the armour plates started to slide into place with a great clanking noise. Pretty soon Keller was standing in front of a fully-dressed Bellori soldier.

'How does it feel?' he asked.

'Tight,' came Ayl's reply through the helmet. His voice sounded a lot deeper.

'Now you, Keller,' said Dray. 'Try to hold your stomach in.'

'What do you mean?' asked the trade prince. He knew he wasn't exactly in shape, but his belly wasn't that big, was it? He just liked his food.

Dray shook her head as she helped him into his armour. She did the straps up and pulled them tight around his chest.

'Easy,' he half-joked. 'I still need to breathe.' He felt the machinery writhing against his back like a nest of dry eels, adjusting itself to his frame. When the Bellori stepped away, he pressed his head back like Ayl had done. The heavy plating swung round instantly and gripped his limbs and torso firmly. More parts squirmed against his body, squeezing and pressing, making itself skin-tight. It was like being swallowed by some giant amoeba.

The helmet swung into place and for an instant he thought the suit was trying to throttle him. He fell to his knees and tried to grab the face plate, pushing it up, gasping for breath. Dray was trying to shake his shoulders and get his attention.

'Relax!' she shouted. 'It's normal! Slow, deep breaths.'

He focused on her words, standing up slowly. 'I think I've got it,' he said.

When he tried to take a step, the suit seemed to push his legs and he almost fell. He had to wave his arms about to keep his balance but it chafed his armpits.

Maybe pretending to be General Iccus isn't such a great idea, he thought.

When he looked up, he saw from her face that Dray agreed. 'I'm OK,' he said. 'I just need some practice.'

'Just be careful,' said Dray, as she stepped into her armour. Within a few clicks she was encased in the suit. She moved around the space with an ease that Keller could never hope to match. He'd been having trouble just staying upright, although he could tell Ayl wasn't finding it all that easy. The Aquanth had barely moved.

Suddenly the deck beneath them shook and an alarm started ringing. Dray ran back to the control room and the other two followed as best they could, bumping into the door frame on their way through.

'What now?' muttered Keller.

A harsh male voice was coming over the ship's com. 'This is the Bellori battleship *Karu*, you are in restricted space. Identify yourselves or we will fire.'

14

Ayl was still stumbling to his seat as Dray tried to open a radio channel to the *Karu*.

'I repeat,' came the man's voice over the coms. 'Identify yourself or we will fire. You have five clicks.'

'Battleship,' said the general's daughter, 'this is a classified flight. We will only report to High Command.'

'What are you doing?' hissed Keller, switching the microphone off.

'Bluffing,' replied the girl. 'Unless you have a better idea.'

The speakers inside the helmet made everything sound far away to Ayl. He tried to turn his head to see what the others were doing and the suit rubbed painfully against his gills. Instinctively, the folds on his neck tried to open, but the armour pinched them shut. He hissed in pain and sat as upright as he could, holding himself still.

'Authentication code,' demanded the *Karu*'s

commander. Dray replied by tapping away at a keyboard to one side of her seat. After a moment, the man's voice came over the radio again. 'Accepted. You are clear to proceed.'

'Thank you, *Karu*,' said Dray and shut down the coms system. 'We're through. Thank the stars Sudor hasn't cancelled my father's codes yet.' She turned her bulk round to face the Cantorian. 'Keller, you should fly us down to the surface. I'm not sure how well this shuttle will deal with atmospheric entry.'

'No problem, sarge,' said Keller as they squeezed past each other to change seats. Ayl could tell that the Cantorian was smiling beneath his helmet. 'Uh, but I thought,' he put on a deep voice, '*it's Bellori*.'

'It's also old,' she replied.

Ayl wondered once again if he was really cut out for spaceflight. He closed his eyes and said a prayer. When he opened his eyes, Bellus filled the view-screens.

It was a smaller planet than Aquanthis, and infinitely drier. From orbit, it didn't look like there was a single drop of water anywhere. Just a barren, red surface. It looked entirely lifeless and Ayl found it hard to believe that a race of people called it their home. He knew from his studies that it was a harsh, unforgiving place. But then this was the world that had made the galaxy's greatest warriors after all.

'Uh, chief,' said Keller, 'I've got all kinds of warning lights flashing . . .'

'Just keep it steady,' said Dray. 'Don't worry, this ship was designed to survive a war.'

'Is this wise?' asked Ayl, trying not to let the worry into his voice.

'There is no other way,' answered the Bellori.

'Outstanding,' muttered the Trade Prince. 'We come all this way just to turn into a heavily armoured firework.'

The ship started shaking violently the instant they hit the atmosphere, the bottom half of the view-screen quickly turning bright red. Ayl felt his stomach lurch. He fought to control it, not wanting to find out what would happen if he was sick with the helmet on. Lights started flashing on the consoles nearest to him.

'You're coming in too steep,' shouted Dray.

'Give me a click,' the Trade Prince replied. 'Firing retros . . . now!'

Ayl was thrown forwards in his seat. His chin hit his chest and he bit deeply into his lip, the blood filling his mouth.

'Engine one just cut out!' yelled the Bellori, and suddenly they were weightless, the whole ship falling.

The piercing shrill of an alarm hurt his ears.

'Switching to engine two,' Keller called out. The ship lurched again and they were all thrown back in their seats. There was a huge thunder-clap behind them and another siren, louder than the first, started ringing.

'Engine two just exploded!' cried Dray.

'I think I can glide us in,' shouted the Cantorian. 'It's going to be bumpy!'

Turbulence shook Ayl to the core as he watched the ground approach on the view-screen. It rushed towards them sickeningly fast. Suddenly he could make out the line of a runway, then the lights down the centre and short buildings on either side. They slammed into the surface and he held on to the arms of his seat with all his strength. A high-pitched screeching sound filled the cabin as they skidded along. After what felt like forever they slowed and finally came to a shuddering halt.

They had arrived on Bellus.

'What a rush,' whispered Keller. He was glad neither of his friends could see his hands – he could feel them shaking as he let go of the control stick. He turned round to look at the two armour-suited figures behind him. 'Another amazing landing, even if I do say so myself.'

'Good work,' said Dray, although she didn't sound as impressed as he'd hoped. Ayl just sat there, perfectly still. The trade prince remembered the first time he'd flown with the Aquanth. He'd bet his trust fund the other boy was trying not to vomit.

It wasn't long before there was a voice over the com-system again, this time a ground-based security commander demanding to know who they were. The three of them walked out on to the runway and came face-to-face with a squad of huge Bellori soldiers. Nine large and complicated-looking rifles were pointing straight at them. The commander, the biggest of the lot, stepped forward. High above their heads, lightning flashed.

'Give me your report,' the warrior demanded.

'We are under orders to report only to High Command,' Dray barked back. Keller was impressed that the girl could sound so confident. Even in her armour she barely came up to the other Bellori's shoulders. Even if she was as scared as he was, she wasn't about to let anybody else know it.

'I am Major Dorn, commander of the First Cohort,' the soldier's voice boomed. 'Give me your report.'

'You have our authentication codes,' said Keller, remembering how his father dealt with all the petty officials back at home. 'Take us to High Command, now!' He shouted the last word, enjoying being able to order a Bellori warrior around and hoping it would work. The huge man looked down at him for a moment.

'Come then,' said Dorn, and turned to lead them into a metal hatchway in a nearby bunker. The trade prince couldn't resist looking at Dray and Ayl and shrugging his shoulders, the closest he could get to a grin in the armour. The girl shook her head as the squad surrounded them and they all filed after the major.

After only a couple of steps, Keller felt exhausted. He'd forgotten about the high gravity on Bellus and the armour made his legs feel like they weighed a tonne. His chest seemed much heavier too, and he struggled to pull down enough to breathe. He didn't even want to think about how Ayl was doing. The Aquanth was weak enough anyway, and Keller hoped he could make it inside without collapsing. Concentrating on putting one foot in front of another, Keller struggled to keep up with Dray and felt sweat drip down the back of his neck.

They walked down long stretches of wide, rock-walled corridors. Metal blast doors and frequent security cameras were all that broke the monotony. Occasionally Keller saw pairs of soldiers standing guard outside a room. The trade prince was glad they had plenty of space, because he was moving clumsily in the bulky suit. He was trying hard to act the part of a Bellori warrior, trying to put some swagger in his walk, but he kept bumping into Ayl.

After an eternity of unmarked passageways, they found themselves standing in front of a huge carbotanium door. In tall letters the words HIGH COMMAND were painted on its surface.

The massive door opened slowly. The dark chamber beyond was a hive of activity. Dozens of soldiers were sat in front of terminals that displayed everything from fleet positions to supply quotas. Runners carried dataslates full of reports from desk to desk. And above it all was the council, the High Command. The five highest ranking and most respected warriors, apart from General Iccus himself. They were perfectly still, like hulking statues, watching over the military machine below, the perfect examples of discipline. Seated at a table on a wide dais, large wall-screens on the opposite wall gave them an overview of everything on the planet and beyond.

Inside his helmet, the trade prince grinned. *I'll wager my last credit that I'm the first Cantorian to see this*, he thought.

* * *

The last time she'd been here, her father had ordered Dray not to speak. He'd been introducing Sudor to the military council and he hadn't wanted her to ruin it for him. She'd hated every moment of it, but she'd stood by his side and done her duty. Now it was her turn, and she relished being at the centre of all things Bellori.

The council were studying a holo-map of the Trinity System, visors raised as they squinted at the spot where Aquanthis should have been. Instead of a planet, there was only empty space.

'It can't have just disappeared! There must be a problem with our satellite signals,' said one of the generals.

Dray stepped into the small area of clear space in front of the council and paused for a beat as the five warriors turned to look at her. Taking a deep breath, she tapped the helmet control with her chin and the whole head-piece swung back, revealing her face to everyone there.

'I am Dray,' she said, with as much authority as she could muster. 'Daughter of General Iccus. I have come to warn the High Command of a new threat.'

Suddenly there was a sharp blow to Dray's back and she was knocked to her knees. Dorn was standing over her, holding his rifle against her head.

'You were last seen fleeing from the conference,' said the major, his voice full of scorn. 'Cowards have no right to be here.'

'Is that what Sudor told you?' she asked, ignoring the soldier and looking up at the council. 'Would a coward walk in here and declare themselves?'

'You shame your father. I should—' shouted the First Cohort's commander.

'Silence,' boomed the deep voice of one of the Bellori leaders. 'The girl will speak.'

'But—' started Dorn, turning to the older warriors.

'The girl will speak,' repeated the other man. The major stepped aside after a moment.

'Thank you, sir,' said Dray, getting up from her knees and standing to attention. 'It is the conference that I must tell you about. We were attacked.'

'By whom?' boomed one of the council.

'By aliens,' she replied. 'Giant insects, as big as a man but deadly. They overwhelmed our security forces. Only I escaped.'

'Why did you not stay and fight with your father?' demanded another one of the five.

'We were separated,' said the girl. 'My first duty was to Bellus. To get out a warning. The insects, they call

152

themselves the Nara-Karith. They plan to attack the three worlds. The Aquanths are already in hiding. We must be ready or all will be lost.'

For a moment, the room was silent. Then the sound of slow clapping came from behind her and she turned to see a familiar figure approaching. The huge warrior walked towards her, flanked by a personal guard of heavily armed troopers.

'And just how did *you* come by this so-called enemy's battle plans?' asked Sudor scathingly.

'I – I . . . can't say,' said Dray.

15

This is not *good*, thought Keller. *Either she tells them about the Aquanths' telepathic powers, or we might never get them on our side.*

He watched as Sudor walked up and stood before the High Command alongside Dray. The captain was quite a lot bigger than her and his chest was bristling with medals and ribbons from past victories. Compared to the general's daughter in her second-hand armour, he looked like a lord of war.

'This child fled from the conference,' Sudor said, addressing the council. 'She abandoned her father out of cowardice. She then disobeyed a direct order and almost caused damage to a Bellori battleship in an asteroid field.'

'He's twisting the truth!' shouted Dray. 'Everything I did, I did for Bellus!'

'Then tell us where you get your information!' Sudor bellowed at her.

The trade prince could see Dray clenching her fists and for a moment it looked like the girl was going to attack. Instead, she took a long look at Ayl, who nodded, then turned back to the council. When she spoke, she was quieter, more deliberate.

'Today I have learnt many things,' she said. 'I have been working with an Aquanth. The blue-bloods have been hiding their true nature from us. They are telepaths. A race of mind readers. My contact was able to see into the aliens' minds. These Nara-Karith may have many bodies, but only one consciousness controls them all and they are all the more deadly for it.'

The five old warriors sitting on the dais just stared stonily at her.

'You are a disgrace,' hissed Sudor. 'Did you really think we would believe that? Telepathy! Ridiculous—' He stopped suddenly, as though something had occurred to him. 'When you fled before, you had two companions. An Aquanth and a Cantorian. Where are they?' He barked the question.

Keller's stomach filled with ice as Sudor turned towards him. He could see the look of horror on Dray's face as the bigger man approached, but there was nothing she could do. Sudor seized the trade prince's helmet and, with two huge hands, wrenched it round and tore it clean away from the suit's neck. The Cantorian heard the council gasp, and felt the cold air of the room hit his skin as the suit started opening. Armour plates pulled back with a heavy clanking sound, leaving him completely exposed and surrounded by Bellori soldiers.

The five council members were standing now, with looks of abject horror on their faces as Sudor opened Ayl's armour, then Dray's. The three friends were forced to their knees and the trade prince found himself looking up at the wide barrel of a guard's plasma rifle.

'This is sacrilege!' Sudor shouted at Dray. 'Not only did you reveal our deepest secret to outsiders but you tried to hide them in our midst!' He swung his arm and slammed the back of his fist into her face. The girl looked dazed for a moment then spat blood at him. 'Council,' he said, addressing the High Command now. 'At the very least she is a traitor to our people. She may well be a spy as well. She must be dealt with!'

'Revealing the secret of the armour,' pronounced the deep voice of one of the Bellori leaders, 'is the highest treason.'

'Espionage is punishable only by death,' came the voice of another.

'She is Iccus's daughter,' said a third.

'She came here of her own free will,' said a fourth.

'Take them to the prison cells,' said the last one in disgust.

Before he could stop himself, Keller was on his feet shouting. 'I am the Trade Prince of—' A soldier slammed his rifle butt hard into the back of the Cantorian's head. The next thing he knew, he was being dragged down a dark corridor by his feet.

Ayl hugged his knees to his chest tightly to stop himself shivering. He was sitting on the ground in the corner of the prison cell watching Dray pace and Keller rub his head.

The room wasn't very big, a little smaller than his bedroom at temple-school. It was cold and dark too, the only light a small bulb above the door. The rough rock of the walls and ceiling offered even less comfort than the dirt under foot. And there wasn't the slightest hint of moisture. He tried to remember the last time he'd been in water. His skin felt itchy and sore and his lungs were starting to sting. He wasn't used to breathing air for so long. What he wouldn't give for even a short swim.

'Krack!' Dray yelled suddenly, slamming her fist into the door. 'What are we going to do?'

'Stop shouting?' suggested Keller with a weak smile. 'I've got a major headache, thank you very much.'

'Sorry,' said the Bellori. 'But we have to do something. And we don't know how much time we have.'

'What *can* we do?' said the trade prince. 'We're locked in a prison cell with no weapons or equipment. They're hardly going to let us live now that we know their little secret.' He grunted in pain and brought his palm up to his forehead.

Ayl had never been knocked out. From the look on the other boy's face, he guessed that it wasn't a pleasant experience.

'My father would know what to do,' growled Dray. 'No one ever stood in his way.'

'Except for my father,' laughed Keller. 'He could argue his way out of anything. Even jail probably.'

'Perhaps we should ask them,' said Ayl, realizing how much he missed his mother. He pulled his legs closer to his body as he looked up at the other two. 'I am almost certain they are still alive.'

'Can you speak to them?' asked Keller, wide-eyed. The Aquanth had a feeling the other boy still didn't quite believe he was telepathic.

'If you are quiet, I will try,' he replied. The other two nodded and Ayl closed his eyes. He tried to slowly block out all physical sensation, focusing on extending his consciousness back out to the asteroid. He felt his being stretch out as it had before, but he was weak and tired. The further he went, the thinner he felt, insubstantial like a line of mist.

He opened his eyes, exhausted, and took a deep breath. 'I don't have the strength,' he said, looking at the other two. Dray turned away in frustration but Keller leaned in towards him.

'Can we help?' asked the trade prince, quietly.

'No,' said Ayl quickly, shocked at the idea. 'That would mean sharing minds, linking ourselves.' He'd looked into Tudeno's thoughts back on Terrial One, but that was different. He wasn't even sure it was technically possible to share minds with them.

'Dray's right,' the Cantorian said softly. 'We need to do something.'

'Mind-sharing between species has never been done,' said Ayl, as temple doctrine bubbled away beneath his thoughts. 'It's forbidden.'

'You wore Bellori armour today,' said Dray. 'That was forbidden.'

Ayl looked at the other two. For his whole life, he had thought of them as the lesser races. There were those at home who believed they weren't as evolved as the Aquanths, were worth less in the cosmic order. Their distance from The Divine supposedly proved them to be more animal than intelligent. But these were his friends.

'Come,' he said. 'You must empty your mind.'

Dray sat cross-legged on the floor with her eyes shut. Ayl had told her that she needed to relax and she was doing her best. It just wasn't that easy. She'd led them here. They had trusted her to get through to the High Command and where were they now? In a prison cell. But she wouldn't let them down again. *Come on – relax!* she ordered herself.

She started running through a shung-ka routine in her mind, the slow-motion version of the Bellori hand-to-hand combat discipline. At first she imagined performing the moves on Sudor, snapping his bones and throwing him through the air. Then the movements became the important thing and she felt her heart slow as she concentrated. And then someone else was there.

She could sense Ayl, and Keller as well. It was like they were standing in an empty room, but facing away from each other. She couldn't see them or hear them but she knew they were there. They seemed to be moving closer, floating inwards to a common centre. Her being stretched and expanded until it was like a cloud of steam that met the other two clouds and blended together. She felt the Aquanth's clarity of purpose and the Cantorian's wily cunning mix with her determination. She recoiled in shock. Her every thought was there for them to see if they wanted to. Then the trade prince chuckled and suddenly all three of them were laughing.

Ayl took control and guided them. Their shared essence stretched out like a silken ribbon, flying past the prison walls and up through the atmosphere. She twisted and turned through the vacuum, feeling lighter than she ever had before. She marvelled at the stars and the planets through Keller's eyes. She felt Ayl's gills breathing in the great ocean of space. Then suddenly they were at the asteroid.

A giant black wall stood in their way and Ayl asked her for strength. They found a minuscule gap in the wall and Dray summoned all her energy to help push them through. She squeezed and strained and finally burst through, rushing out on to the other side with a cry of victory.

The asteroid was alive. Flames flowed in every direction and at its centre a giant fireball burned as bright as a star. The Aquanth wasn't distracted, though. He drove them onwards, as they searched for their parents.

Three coloured lights appeared near the middle of the mass and suddenly a bright blue light enveloped them. In front of them stood the high priestess.

My son, exclaimed Lady Moa.

Dray was immediately overcome with joy. *I can feel their emotions*, she thought.

We all can, came the voice of the trade prince from somewhere inside her mind.

Mother, Ayl said, *I thought I would never see you again*. Dray was amazed by the warmth between them. It was nothing like how she felt towards her father.

You have brought friends, said the high priestess, puzzled. She probed Dray and Keller's minds before either had a chance to react. *They care for you.*

You must help us, Ayl said. *What should we do?*

The Nara-Karith are almost ready to attack, said the woman, her calm like a shield. Lady Moa was hiding them from whatever was in charge of the Nara-Karith, but her strength was failing. The blue light was flickering, and a hot, angry presence loomed just beyond. *Kill the queen*, the high priestess shouted over a new noise. There seemed to be a million insects scratching at the blue walls now. *Without her the hive will fall into chaos—*

A terrible, scalding pain erupted in every crevice of Dray's mind. She screamed in agony as she flew through space and back into her body. She lay on the floor, struggling to breathe, checking her body for burns that weren't there.

A heavy clanking sound came from the door and she turned to see a fully armoured Bellori guard walk in.

'Get up, traitor,' the warrior said. 'It's time to die.'

16

'Easy,' yelled Keller as a guard grabbed him by the shoulder, dragging him to his feet. 'I can stand by myself, you great mullock!'

The soldier gave him a hard shove and he was sent stumbling through the cell door and out into the corridor. Six more of the Bellori were standing outside, waiting for him and his friends. The trade prince could feel his heart hammering away in his chest. He still felt hot and feverish from whatever it was that had happened during the mind-sharing, but it was fading, being replaced by a sense of impending doom. It was just all so ridiculous. He was royalty, the heir to an entire world, and here he was being pushed around by a bunch of thugs!

'Nine soldiers?' he asked one of the guards, starting to laugh. 'Are you that scared of three unarmed teenagers?' He put up his fists in a parody of a boxing stance. The warrior gave him a hard stare, but didn't reply. Dray and Ayl had been brought out now as well, and the three of them were marched down the wide corridor flanked by the armed men.

'Maybe it isn't you that's scared,' said Keller, grinning up at the nearest guard. 'Maybe Sudor just doesn't think you're good enough to handle us, so that's why he had to send so many of you.' He thought he saw the guard flinch for a moment. The idea that he was getting to one of his executioners, winding him up, cured any fear. 'I'm almost embarrassed to be killed by such sub-standard troops.'

'I'm told that aggravating Bellori warriors is not a good idea,' Ayl whispered to his friend. The Aquanth looked worried, but Keller wasn't about to let some brute think he had the Trade Prince of Cantor scared.

'What are they going to do, Ayl?' he asked. 'Kill us some more? We're already on the way to our execution.' The other boy opened his mouth to speak again, but he didn't have any answer. There were huge bags under the Aquanth's eyes and he was walking stiffly. Keller guessed he just didn't have the energy to argue. Dray, on the other hand, was all eyes and ears. She moved like a cat, ready to spring on the smallest chance of escape. *Not that there is any chance*, he thought.

Another troop of Bellori were passing and Keller

pointed to them, turning to talk to the guard again. 'What about them?' he asked, mock serious. 'I bet they're heading off to fight a real enemy, win a famous victory or something. But you? No way, shoot a kid in the back instead, much safer.'

'I'm warning you, boy,' said the guard quietly, without turning his head. The warrior might have thought he was being menacing, but Keller knew he had the advantage now. Getting a response just showed he'd found the man's weak spot.

'And what about job satisfaction?' the Cantorian asked. 'I thought you Bellori were all about honour in battle? Executing children? We can't even fight back! Are you going to get your friends to hold us down while you shoot?'

The guard turned suddenly and grabbed hold of Keller with a hand that felt like it could crush rock.

'Sounds like a job for a coward to me!' Keller shouted right into the soldier's face. The guard brought up his weapon and aimed it straight at the Cantorian's chest. Willing himself not to flinch, Keller goaded him – 'Go on, then!'

Instead of the explosion he expected, Keller heard a strange gurgling sound. The guard slumped to his knees, falling flat on his face and revealing a large, smouldering hole in his back. The trade prince looked up to see one of the passing Bellori standing in front of him, dirty smoke rising from the barrel of the plasma rifle in his hands.

Dray grabbed both of her friends and pulled them to the ground as the two squads of Bellori opened fire on each other. A barrage of heat roared over their heads and the bodies of the guards fell in a circle around them. It was all over in a few clicks and, when she looked up, all of their would-be executioners were dead. Standing in front of her was a big warrior reloading a heavy bolt-rifle with bullets. As he slapped in the magazine, his helmet folded back to reveal his face.

'Come with me if you want to live,' said Tudeno, pulling back the bolt on his weapon and sending a round into the chamber with a satisfying *clunk*. The rest of his squad stood ready behind him.

'I thought you weren't coming,' said Keller breathlessly.

The old warrior looked at him for a moment. 'We have a ship,' he replied. 'We can get you to safety.'

'But how did you get into Bellori airspace?' Dray asked.

'The High Command were too busy dealing with

you to pay much attention to our ship,' said Tudeno with a faint smile.

'Thank you,' said Dray, simply. The man just nodded. She knew how much honour meant to men like Tudeno – it meant just as much to her after all. He had broken an oath to help her and she would never forget it.

He held out the bolt-rifle to Dray along with an ammunition belt. She took the weapon and turned to Keller and Ayl. 'We're going to have to fight all the way to the ship,' she said. 'Stay close to me. Are you ready?'

The Cantorian and the Aquanth turned to each other for a moment and both of the boys tensed their jaws. She almost laughed at how similar they looked with identical grimaces.

'We're ready,' said Ayl.

'Right behind you,' said the trade prince, trying to smile.

Another squad of Bellori troopers burst into the corridor only a few yards away. They fired off a few shots before a bolt of plasma from one of Tudeno's men decimated them. The three friends were up and running immediately, following the exiles as they powered through the passageway. Their rescuers surrounded them, just as the guards had done before, but this time issuing forth a devastating barrage of fire on anyone who tried to attack.

Dray felt energized. After all the sitting around and the talking and the waiting, this was what she needed. A good, honest, old-fashioned fire-fight. There was no confusion in her mind. This was what she'd been born for.

A combat drone flew out of an air-duct up ahead and swivelled in mid-air, bringing two particle-lasers to bear on her. She raised her weapon and pulled the trigger, relishing the kick in her shoulder from the recoil. The drone exploded in a cloud of smoke and sparks.

At an intersection she roared as she fired shot after shot around a corner, covering the boys as they got past. She grabbed a dead soldier's grenade launcher and fired both weapons at an oncoming squad of Bellori, pouring a lifetime of rage and frustration into the fight. Dray had been waiting all her life for this moment, but never thought it would be her own people that she'd be fighting against.

At last they made it to the gigantic hangar bay, big enough for a battleship. The space was empty apart from the exiles' shuttle, parked in the middle of the cavernous room.

Nearly out of here, thought Dray, as the group sprinted to the spacecraft, *just a few more paces to go—*

A huge pressure wave knocked her down before the sound of an explosion reached her. Dray looked up to see a fire-ball rising from where the ship had been and dozens of Bellori soldiers charging out of the entrances on either side of the hangar.

All hope of escaping from Bellus had just gone up in flames.

Large chunks of debris from the shuttle started to fall around them. They were pinned down and completely surrounded. Ayl knelt behind a piece of wreckage with his hands over his ears.

Beside him, Dray used a section of burnt metal as a shield and opened fire at the nearest enemy squad. Ayl watched as Dray's rifle spat shiny silver cylinders in an arc out of its side. She gritted her teeth, concentrating on putting out as many bullets as possible.

All around them, laser beams and bolts of plasma were searing through the air as the enemy returned fire. Ayl saw a shot catch one of Tudeno's men. The exile jerked backwards with the force of the blow and fell, instantly dead. Ayl squeezed his eyes shut to block out the horror.

Then there was a sudden silence. The gunfire had stopped. Ayl peeked out to see a huge Bellori striding towards them. It was Sudor.

'Dray,' the gigantic warrior called out. 'Surrender. You have no choice.'

The General's daughter tightened her grip on the bolt-rifle and started to stand up. The Aquanth quickly put his hand out and tried to pull her down, to keep her behind the metal debris that protected them. She looked at him for a moment and he remembered the strength he'd felt when they'd shared minds. He knew he'd never stop her – nothing would, not even Sudor. She looked right back at him and smiled. Then she handed him her gun and walked towards her enemy unarmed and unarmoured.

Ayl crouched down and watched her go, hoping he could shoot if he needed to.

'Surrender now, traitor,' shouted Sudor, grandstanding in front of the troops. 'Before you get more real Bellori killed.'

'You brought us to this, Sudor,' Dray replied, loudly enough for everyone in the huge space to hear. 'And I know what you're doing.'

'Trying to save our race from your treachery, *child*,' he almost spat the last word. 'You have broken our most sacred laws.'

'I have fought to save our people!' she replied. She was face to face with the armoured giant now, and she looked tiny in comparison. But her voice carried, and everyone could see her standing up to this behemoth. 'You are holding back the Bellori! You won't attack the aliens because you want my father to die so that you can take power!'

'Lies!' Sudor roared, turning away.

'You are too scared to challenge him for the leadership,' Dray was roaring now, demanding attention. 'You are a coward, Sudor!'

The huge warrior spun round and struck her across the face with the edge of his armour-plated hand. Dray went flying backwards, the blow sending an arc of blood spurting from her face. The hangar went silent and Ayl didn't need to be a telepath to feel the shock all of the Bellori in the room. Their leader had struck an unarmed opponent, a terribly dishonourable act.

Dray slowly stood up and wiped the blood from her lips. She raised a hand and pointed at her enemy. 'Blood challenge,' she said, almost too quietly for Ayl to hear. There was a collective gasp from the Bellori, audible despite their helmets.

'You . . . you can't . . .' muttered Sudor, sounding

unsure and stepping back from the girl. He twisted around, looking for support from the watching soldiers.

'I call for a blood challenge,' repeated Dray, loud enough to reach everyone this time. 'You and me, Sudor. For the Bellori leadership. To the death.'

17

'You challenge me?' thundered Sudor, his surprise forgotten. 'That's impossible. It's illegal. You're just a child!' There was a murmur in the ranks of the soldiers behind him. They went silent as Keller ran to stand by his friend.

'You're lying,' said the trade prince, looking up at Dray's adversary. The man was even bigger up close.

'What did you say to me, Cantorian?' roared Sudor. Keller's lunch wanted to jump out of his throat, but he forced it to stay down and went on.

'You're a liar,' he said again. He turned to the crowd of soldiers. 'There is nothing in your law to prevent this blood challenge! The only reason for refusal is cowardice! Do you follow a coward?' The enemy soldiers muttered among themselves, but the trade prince could hear the exiles behind him, cheering.

'What do you know about our laws, shopkeeper?' snapped Sudor.

'I have studied your customs. A shopkeeper must know his customers, after all,' Keller replied, trying to keep his voice from breaking.

'Fight me,' Dray spat the words at the older man. 'Or are you too scared?'

At that the exiles pounded their chests in approval. Keller could see what was going on. Everyone, even those fighting against her, must have been impressed by Dray's courage. This girl, standing before this warlord, without even her armour or a weapon, had the respect of the crowd. It was up to Sudor now, to show everyone he deserved to lead.

'Challenge accepted,' the man said. Then he raised his arms and shouted to the crowd. 'Blood challenge!'

The ranks of soldiers roared their approval, clapping and stamping in a riot of noise. Groups of warriors quickly cleared debris from the centre of the hangar. The rest started to move into a rough circle – a makeshift arena.

'Cantorian,' Sudor said quietly, towering over the trade prince, 'when this is over, I'm coming for you.'

'When this is over,' Keller replied, with as big a grin as he could manage, 'I'll sell your armour for scrap.' The man growled at him then stalked off towards his troops.

'Come on, tough guy,' said Dray, punching the boy on the arm and forcing a smile. The two of them walked back and stood with Ayl and Tudeno. One of the exiles brought her a new suit of armour and a huge, two-handed sword. She tested the weapon, swinging it through the air.

'You don't need to do this,' said the Aquanth, looking worried. 'There must be another way.' Dray grimaced, then handed him the blade. It was so heavy that the blue-skinned boy almost dropped it, his eyes going wide in surprise.

'I have trained for this my entire life,' she said. 'If I win, we three will lead the Bellori into battle together. If I lose, the Nara-Karith will overrun the worlds. There is no choice.'

She stepped backwards into the armour and Keller watched as the sections closed around her.

'Good luck,' he said, looking straight into her eyes. Then the helmet closed over her face. She took her weapon and stepped out to face Sudor.

'I've been waiting a long time for this, *girl*,' said Sudor, as Dray stepped into the circle. He looked huge in his armour, with a gigantic sword held loosely at his side. He swung the weapon round and up in an elaborate salute, showing off his skills. This was it. The chance to prove to the world she was a warrior.

'We should have done this a long time ago,' answered Dray, simply lifting her blade straight up in reply to his salute. She moved into a fighting posture and the two combatants circled each other. How many practice bouts had she worked through, pretending her opponent was this cretin?

'Your father would never allow it,' said the older man, laughing mirthlessly. She watched his blade as it weaved through the air. 'He always said you were too delicate. Not a real Bellori.'

'You talk too much,' she spat. 'Come at me!' She let her longsword drop slightly to one side, giving him an opening.

'So be it!' yelled Sudor. Suddenly his immense blade was swinging through the air at her newly exposed flank. Exactly as she'd planned.

She leapt to the right and brought her weapon up in a long slice. Sudor jumped back but the cutting edge of her weapon gouged a line into his chest plate. His fist shot out, slamming into her shoulder, and sent her staggering back. She dodged just as the point of Sudor's weapon stabbed through the air where her head had been. They started circling each other again, wary now.

'It'll take more than that, child,' hissed Sudor. He stepped towards her and his weapon slashed down at her from above. She parried and the blades clanged together. The shock travelled along her sword and straight into the shoulder he'd smacked before. She cried out in pain and her enemy laughed.

She made a stab at his neck and he leaned backwards, off balance, to avoid it. She slashed at his arms, but he blocked. They exchanged blow after blow, moving around each other, sword ringing against sword. He was so much stronger, each of his attacks felt like a sledgehammer strike. She tried to work her way in closer and closer, get inside his reach. She wasn't as powerful, but she had speed and accuracy on her side. Her arms were getting heavier by the moment and she jigged aside, skipping backwards to get some space to breathe.

'Getting tired?' he asked, moving into the attack again.

'You've already lost,' she shouted at her enemy.

Sudor looked round at the crowd for approval, but all that could be heard were low mutters. This was her chance. Dray darted forward, her blade slicing low at the knee joint. He parried too late and was off balance again. She followed with a volley of quick stabs, forcing him back. The man didn't have the speed to defend properly and was left flailing. He yelled in desperation and brought his foot up in a fierce kick to the chest, knocking her away and driving the wind from her lungs.

'This is my time!' roared Sudor. He swung his colossal sword up over his head and brought it down double-handed in a massive blow that took all her strength to ward off. The titanic warrior screamed incoherently and starting raining strike after strike down on her. Each blow knocked her back more and more. She didn't have time to think, forcing her blade up to parry again and again. Suddenly her opponent switched his grip and brought the weighted pommel of his sword handle against the flat of her blade. Her arms seemed to spring upwards as it shattered and she was left with only half a weapon.

'My time!' Sudor thundered. He brought the steel up above his head, ready for the killing blow. 'So much for the line of Iccus,' he spat.

But before he could bring the sword down he froze. The crowd was thumping their fists against their armour and shouting, 'Dray! Dray! Dray!' It took a moment for their words to sink in. Dray felt a surge of pride as she realized the soldiers were thundering their approval, urging her to fight back. Not just Tudeno's men, but Sudor's army as well.

Fuelled by the crowd's support, Dray leapt forwards. Dodging the blade, she charged into her opponent, ramming her shoulder into the top of his legs and wrapping her arms around them.

'For Bellus!' she yelled, lifting him up with all of her strength, screaming until her throat was hoarse, feeling every muscle in her body strain. She pushed and pushed forwards, driving Sudor down now, into the ground, trying to pummel him into dust. The huge man lost grip of his sword and the wind was driven out of him. Dray straddled his chest, victorious. She brought the jagged, broken metal shard that was the remains of her sword and placed it at his neck, between the join in his armour. She leaned forwards, ready to apply the pressure that would kill.

A panel on Sudor's shoulder plate slid open and something slid out. Out of the corner of her eye Dray could see the muzzle of a k-gun. Then there was a blinding flash of light, and Dray felt herself being thrown through the air.

Ayl watched as Dray landed on the ground and lay there, unmoving. The crowd was silent, no longer chanting Dray's name. His heart dropped as Sudor slowly stood up. The soldier rolled his shoulders, then stooped to pick up his sword.

'No,' he heard himself whisper.

Dray was stirring now, coming round again, but not quickly enough. Her opponent stood over her and raised his weapon, ready to bring it down in a killing blow and finish the duel. The Aquanth could not believe that it was going to end like this. He wouldn't let it end like this. He ran towards his friend.

'Stop!' he yelled, throwing himself on top of Dray, using his body as a shield. Sudor grabbed him by the neck and threw him aside. Ayl landed a few feet away, the impact jarring his whole body, but jumped up quickly.

'I won't let you hurt her!' he cried, leaping in front of the armoured giant again. The man drove a huge fist into the Aquanth's stomach, sending him flying backwards and forcing the air from his lungs. Ayl fell to his knees taking great gulps of air.

Suddenly Keller was standing next to him, helping him up.

'Where is the honour in this?' the Trade Prince shouted to the onlookers. 'Does it take an Aquanth and a Cantorian to tell the Bellori that this coward cheated?'

Sudor stepped forward and pointed his great sword at the two boys. 'You dare call me a coward, merchant!' growled the older man, looking as though he would kill them in an instant.

'Strike then,' cried out Ayl, struggling for breath. 'Show your soldiers what a warrior you are.'

'This Aquanth has more courage than your leader!' Keller called out to the crowd, who were muttering in disapproval. Ayl could see Dray start to sit up now, but the other boy carried on talking.

'He is not worthy to lead you!' he yelled. 'He has no honour. There is only one who is worthy of being your commander!' He pointed at Dray, as she stood. The assembly thundered as all the warriors bellowed and rushed forward.

For an instant Ayl thought the surging crowd was going to attack Dray. But instead they surrounded Sudor and beat him to the ground. Then the Bellori soldiers lifted Dray on to their shoulders, as if her heavy armour weighed less than a feather. Cries of 'All hail General Dray!' echoed as the Bellori saluted their new leader. Shouting their approval, they carried her on a victory lap around the hangar.

After a few minutes the girl made them set her down and she walked over to where they held her enemy.

Dray looked as if she'd just tasted something rotten as she glared down at her defeated foe. 'Remove your armour,' she ordered Sudor. 'You have forfeited the right to call yourself Bellori.'

Ayl watched as the keratin plates peeled back, and the real Sudor emerged. Even without his armour the man was impressively large. But there was something sharp about him. Burning with humiliation, Sudor's eyes darted about, looking for a way to escape. For a moment the boy felt sorry for him, this broken man. But only for a moment.

Ayl made his way through the crowd to stand next to his friends. 'What are you going to do with him?' he asked. The crowd had gone quiet, everyone waiting for her to pass judgement.

'It was a blood challenge,' said Keller. 'The law says he should die.'

'He doesn't deserve that escape,' replied Dray. 'Let him live with his dishonour.' She held her hands up. 'Exile for the loser,' she shouted, and another great cheer rose from the gathered soldiers.

Two warriors that Ayl recognized as Tudeno's men came forward and dragged Sudor away, giving him a few kicks for good measure. Dray took hold of the Aquanth and the Cantorian's hands and held them aloft.

'These are our allies,' she yelled, calling out to everyone who could hear. 'These are my comrades. There is a new enemy to fight! Assemble the fleet – we are going to WAR!'

18

Dray couldn't believe what had happened. She'd been fighting for her life barely an hour ago, facing execution as a traitor to Bellus. Now she was in command of a Bellori battle-cruiser, en route to the asteroid.

News of her victory had spread through the data-nets like wildfire and the entire planet had rallied to support her. Ayl had called it a miracle, but she couldn't help thinking it was fate. At any rate, she promised herself a visit to one of Aquanthis's temples when this was all over.

Keller and Ayl were watching the view-screen as the communications officer set up a holo-link with the fleet commanders. When the lieutenant made the connection and nodded to her, she led the other two into the conference chamber. It was time to make a battle plan.

'So what next, General?' asked the Cantorian, smirking. Apparently he found her new rank amusing. But now wasn't the time for jokes.

'We're going to end this,' she replied. She was still wearing her armour but she had the visor up so she could talk to them without any obstruction. The room they entered held a long metal table and she sat at one end, ready to take charge of the discussion. Her two friends sat to either side of her.

'A better question might be how?' said Ayl. There was a quiet authority about the boy now. He'd managed to have a quick soak in the ship's water tank when they'd come aboard and emerged rejuvenated – his skin once again a lustrous blue.

Before she could answer, eight more Bellori figures materialized around the table. These were the admirals of the fleet, able to order thousands of combat troops into action. The holograms were good, but not perfect, and the images shook and crackled throughout the discussion.

'We are here to find a way to destroy the alien threat,' said Dray, taking charge instantly. 'The Nara-Karith are confined at the moment, but this will not last forever.'

'Bombard the asteroid,' replied one of the officers curtly. 'We have the firepower to completely destroy it.'

'No.' Keller slapped his hand on the table and looked at his friends. 'Our parents are still trapped there. We can't abandon them.'

'It's the only way to be sure,' the Bellori commander growled. The other holograms all muttered their approval. 'We don't know enough about the aliens to attempt a rescue.'

It was a simple tactical equation: sacrifice the few to save the many. Dray felt her heart drop. She might be in charge of the greatest fighting force known to the galaxy, but that meant she was now responsible for billions of civilians too.

'We kill the queen,' said Keller, and he suddenly had a glint in his eye. 'If we kill her, the aliens will descend into chaos. We can rescue my father. The high priestess and General Iccus too.'

'And just *how* do you intend to get through the alien's defences?' said a different admiral, leaning forward. Dray picked up on his tone, patronising to the point of arrogance. She would deal with him later.

'Perhaps I can help with that,' said the Aquanth.

Keller wasn't sure if Ayl had just winked at him – he was still getting used to the whole double-eyelid thing – but he was glad the Aquanth was helping. For a moment there he'd thought he might have to accept defeat. That would have meant the end for his father, and he wasn't ready to be trade king yet. Not by a long way.

'I believe I can conceal a small ship,' said the other boy, his quiet voice commanding attention. 'I have been thinking about the psychic barrier the priests created around Aquanthis. I cannot create anything of the same scale, but, perhaps, something large enough for a shuttle.'

'Impossible,' scoffed one of the Bellori, looking straight at Dray, an old-school general with a chest covered in medals. 'We've been trying to develop a cloaking shield for over ten turns with no success.' In a voice laden with scorn, he asked, 'You really think this child, this seaweed-eater, can make one all on his own?'

'Careful. He is no younger than I,' growled Dray, staring at the man until he looked away. 'This Aquanth has shown himself capable of incredible things. Can you really do this, Ayl?' asked Dray.

'I believe so, yes,' replied the Aquanth.

'I will ready an assault craft with shock troops immediately,' said the officer who had first spoken.

'No,' said Ayl. 'I must go as well, if I am to make the shield.'

'There's no way you're leaving me behind,' Keller was surprised to hear himself say. So here it was. His father had told him that he'd talk himself into real trouble one day. And demanding a place on an assault ship heading for an asteroid infested with giant killer bugs certainly fitted the bill.

'And I will lead the squad,' said Dray. Her tone was clear: there wasn't going to be any argument. 'There should be space for six more troopers. We will need your best.'

A few more minutes and the plan was set. They would have two hours to get in and get out. After that, the fleet would open fire and anything bigger than a microbe would be blown apart. One by one the holograms shut down and the three friends were left alone again.

Keller smirked. 'Back to where it all began, eh? Except that now we know none of us are getting the asteroid.'

Ayl wished he was able to hide a bigger ship, as this one was pretty crowded. He was crammed into the back of the shuttle with six huge Bellori commandos, each with an assortment of guns, rifles, swords and other equipment he didn't even recognize. Dray and Keller were in the forward compartment, piloting the ship. He felt tiny, wearing only a borrowed flight suit, surrounded by these armour-plated soldiers. They were all silent, preparing for the battle ahead in their own way.

He watched as one of the soldiers took out a picture of a young Bellori man and stared at it for a long minute. A corporal couldn't stop tapping his foot, his body brimming with nervous energy. These were the toughest warriors in the galaxy, but they were still people. People with families and friends, people who wanted to get home again. And they were relying on him to keep them safe.

'Ayl, buddy,' Keller's voice came over the intercom suddenly, breaking into his reverie. 'We need you to do your thing. We'll be landing on the asteroid in five minutes.'

'Understood,' replied Ayl, closing his eyes. He'd been trying to remember the exact sensation he'd experienced when Aquanthis had used the Shroud. It had been a rapid disappearance. Although his teachers had never taught him how to do it, he was pretty sure he could produce the same effect.

He concentrated, picturing a strong wall around the shuttle. No, that wasn't quite right – a wall built with his mind alone could never withstand an army of aliens. How could he make them invisible? He cleared his mind and tried to make it completely blank, but it was no use – as long as he was alive, he couldn't completely mask his consciousness.

Maybe the trick wasn't to make them invisible, but to distract whoever might see them so that they looked away. Ayl focused and pictured a clear, shimmering bubble around the ship. Hopefully, the bubble would deflect anyone who looked at it, like light bouncing off a mirror. Of course, if it didn't work, they were about to find themselves in a lot of trouble. *It's a huge gamble*, he thought. *Perhaps I've spent too much time with the Cantorian.*

Ayl felt the ship vibrate as the retro-rockets fired and then a solid clang announced that they'd landed. A hatch in the cabin swung open and the six soldiers filed out quickly with their weapons ready, as smoothly as if they'd practised the manoeuvre a thousand times before. The lack of gunfire only made him feel marginally safer. Dray and Keller walked through the door from the flight deck.

'Whatever happens next, uh . . .' said Keller. The boy looked a little sheepish and Ayl wasn't sure what to expect. 'I just want to say, it's been a privilege knowing you both.'

'Thank you,' said Ayl, bowing slightly to show his respect. 'I am blessed to call you both friends.'

'And I am honoured to fight alongside you,' replied Dray. They all paused for an instant, surprised at just how close they'd become in such a short space of time. Then the Bellori hefted her new k-gun. She worked the pump-action under the barrel as her helmet slid back over her face. She was once again a war-machine. 'Let's go,' she said.

He saw the squad waiting for them as he jogged down the ramp. They'd taken up a defensive formation in the small hangar bay they'd landed in. Two of them were standing ready at an access hatch and they palmed it open as Dray jogged towards them. The corridor beyond was dark, lit only by flickering neon strips along the ceiling. She didn't pause, just brought her weapon up and moved in. The rest of the squad followed.

Ayl found himself alongside the trade prince in the middle of the group as they moved through the conference centre. The general's daughter kept up a good pace, leading them through the metal passageways. The rest of the soldiers seemed to move as a single unit, always keeping two of their number at the back of the group, two at the sides, and two up front with their commander. The place didn't feel as though it had been invaded by aliens. If anything, it felt as though it had just been abandoned. There wasn't any real damage and, best of all, they hadn't seen a single Nara-Karith yet.

'Looks like your shield worked,' said Keller, struggling for breath. The trade prince was a bit red in the face, and Ayl wondered just how often the other boy did any exercise.

'I pray that it has,' replied the Aquanth. 'But how are we going to find our parents now that we're here?'

'Don't you worry about that,' laughed the Cantorian, holding up a data-slate and sounding pleased with himself. 'Did some scans before we landed. There's a tunnel system starting near the main conference chamber. You just let us know if your telepathy starts tingling or something.'

'Quiet,' hissed one of the soldiers, turning towards them. 'This is a stealth mission!'

'Sir, yes, sir!' whispered Keller, nudging the Aquanth with an elbow and winking.

After that they jogged on in silence. Pretty soon the passageways began to widen out and look grander. Thick carpets covered the floor and rich tapestries hung from the walls. Ayl recognized the corridor as one of the thoroughfares he'd used before, between the large hangar-bay and the main chamber.

Then he saw it. Pushed to one side and in the middle of a puddle of blood. A hand, ripped from someone's wrist and discarded. There were more signs of the alien's attack the further they went. Blood spatters and random body parts. Torn furniture and scorch marks from weapon blasts. But no survivors. And still no Nara-Karith. Ayl wished he could be sure that it was because the shield was working. He was struggling to keep it in place; his concentration was slipping.

Finally they came to the entrance of the tunnel. To the high priestess's son it looked like the entrance to the underworld itself. Almost pitch black and sloping downwards, it was a rocky ramp into untold horrors. The mouth was surrounded by jagged, bent back pieces of metal where an explosion had ripped it open. Ayl paused on the threshold, then followed the trade prince down, feeling incredibly vulnerable in the darkness. He heard the warriors of the rearguard coming in behind him and turned to see them silhouetted by the light of the entrance.

Impossibly fast, an insect shape dashed across the mouth of the tunnel and one of the soldiers was dragged away. Ayl yelled and turned to run down into the darkness. Suddenly, there was the rapid flash and bang of a bolt-rifle ahead. In the harsh flickering light he saw the corporal stabbed through the body by a spear-like arm and lifted into the air, screaming.

The Nara-Karith were coming.

19

'What the . . .' yelled Keller as one of the commandos shoved him out of the way. The trade prince hit the wall hard and almost fell. He looked up to see the soldier swing his weapon towards the tunnel entrance.

'Stay down!' yelled the fighter as he opened fire. The multiple barrels on his weapon blurred as they spun round, spitting flame and firing out a blast of energy.

'Watch out,' cried the Cantorian, as a hole opened in the ceiling. A serrated insect leg whipped out and sliced into the Bellori's helmet, decapitating the man. The leg flicked back and the trooper's body slumped to the floor.

'Krack,' muttered Keller, turning round quickly and struggling for breath. 'Krack!'

He watched, frozen still, as a Nara-Karith tried to squeeze its body through the opening. His stomach turned to liquid as the monster stretched towards him. His legs suddenly worked again and he scrambled back until he came up against something hard. He looked up and saw Dray looming over him with her k-gun.

'Need a hand?' she asked, and let off a single shot, reducing the bug to a mess of slime. She dragged him to his feet. 'Come on,' she shouted. 'We have to move.'

'Yeah,' he replied. They stumbled on, further into the tunnel. He bumped into Ayl and pulled the other boy along with him. The sound of the insect followed them, a constant chittering that filled his ears.

'Keep going,' yelled Dray, turning round to fight. She went down on one knee and fired shot after shot.

'Don't be too long,' he called back to her. Up ahead there were two Bellori soldiers, running along the tunnel, firing their weapons at anything that moved. But as they ran, the walls on either side of them crumbled and dozens of the aliens burst out. They rushed the pair of commandos, ripping them to shreds in milliclicks. The Cantorian skidded to a halt. Dray pushed him to one side and threw a small metal ball towards the monsters.

'Get down,' she yelled. Keller grabbed the Aquanth and pulled him to the floor. A moment later a blinding flash of light filled the tunnel and an immense boom shook him to the core. He looked up to see that the tunnel had collapsed, the Nara-Karith crushed beneath tonnes of rock. It was just him, Ayl and Dray now. There was no going back, and a horde of the aliens were charging towards them. Dray knelt and started firing into the mass of insects, keeping them at a distance.

'Come on, Keller,' the trade prince whispered to himself. 'Think of something . . .' He looked down and saw the corpse of one of the soldiers, plasma rifle still in his hands. Keller grabbed the weapon, grunting at the weight as he held it up to his shoulder. He pulled the trigger, and was nearly knocked backwards off his feet as a ball of super-heated gas flew out of the barrel. It hit the roof of the tunnel harmlessly and Keller cursed. He fired blindly into the aliens, which were getting closer by the click. Behind him, he could hear Ayl praying and chanting.

This is it, thought Keller. *I'm going to die*. He kept pulling the trigger, but it didn't seem real. It was like he was playing a holo-game. This wasn't what he was good at, charging about, being a hero. His wars were supposed to be in the marketplace or the boardroom, not on a battlefield.

That's it! These giant, alien bug-things, they were just another business rival. This whole invasion, it was a hostile takeover, more or less. And when a business rival was a lot more powerful than you, you didn't go in all guns blazing. You talked. You talked until you'd found their weak-spot. And then you struck.

Before he could stop himself, Keller had thrown his rifle to the ground and stepped forward with his arms up.

'Wait!' he shouted. 'We surrender!'

'What are you doing?' hissed Dray. The Nara-Karith had suddenly stopped in a line only a few paces away, forming an almost solid wall of insects. They were nearly motionless, only the odd twitch of a spiked leg breaking the stillness and drawing her eye. Like a wave of violence, barely held in check, they were ready to come crashing down on them at any moment.

'Keeping us alive,' Keller whispered back as he stepped forward. He spoke to the aliens next. 'We are the leaders of the three worlds. We can arrange their surrender.'

'Never!' shouted Dray, raising her k-gun again. Keller quickly slapped it down before she could take a shot.

'Trust me,' he said, and winked at her. 'We need to stay alive, and maybe they'll take us to the queen.'

He was right, Dray suddenly realized. The creatures would have to take them to their commander, if that was even the right word. It might not work, but it was worth a shot. Dray dropped her k-gun on the floor and put her hands in the air. Ayl had stepped up to stand by her side now.

'Take us to your leader!' said Keller, turning back to the aliens. He looked over his shoulder at his two friends and there was a huge grin on his face. 'I've always wanted to say that.'

His smile faded as the mass of aliens swarmed around them, closer and closer, forming a circle around the three teenagers. Dray, Keller and Ayl were pushed together until they were all standing back-to-back. Then the insects paused, their huge jaws twitching. 'What are they doing?' Keller hissed to Ayl.

The Aquanth went as still as the bugs, as if he was listening to something. 'It's the queen,' he muttered. 'They're asking her what to do. She – yes, she's telling them to bring us to her.' Keller sighed with relief.

Immediately a group of Nara-Karith started digging at the collapsed section of tunnel with incredible speed, flinging huge lumps of rock aside. Within minutes a space was cleared, and the Bellori, the Cantorian and the Aquanth were ushered forward with prods from harpoon-like alien limbs. Dray went reluctantly, her body tensed for action.

They'd been moving for a while before the rough rock walls of the tunnels changed. At first Dray thought they'd just been smoothed out, but soon there was more light and she could see the difference clearly. The rock looked as though it had been covered in some kind of black resin, glossy and slick. It was a tough version of the creatures' shells, but coated everywhere, on every surface. Large glowing balls stuck out like giant trapped fireflies, flickering as though they had a flame inside. The effect was surreal, tricking the eye into thinking the walls were moving, closing in on them. Dray tried to suppress her unease as they were marched deeper and deeper into the Nara-Karith hive. There was no way they would find their way out of this maze. She wondered if the others knew that they were walking to their deaths.

'How long have we got?' asked Keller, under his breath, snapping Dray out of her reverie.

'One hour and twenty,' she replied, checking the time display inside her helmet. Only eighty minutes until the fleet fired everything they had at them. At least death would be swift. If they survived that long.

'Is that enough time?' whispered Ayl.

'It'll have to be,' the girl answered.

The hive seemed to go on forever, and Dray had

nearly lost track of where they were, when she noticed the temperature spike. Her armour registered a strong breeze blowing towards them. The hot, moist air was powerful enough to blow Keller's hair around and it almost knocked Ayl over. The Aquanth took her arm and she helped him keep moving. The wind cut out quickly as they turned a corner. What they saw stopped them dead in their tracks.

I should have blown this place up when I had the chance, Dray thought.

Ayl stared around at the huge spherical space. The chamber was immense, easily large enough to fit a battleship into, and criss-crossed with pillars of rock. The air was so hot and humid that it felt almost like he was in water. He closed his eyes for an instant and prayed that something had made him hallucinate. When he looked again, he knew it was real.

Almost every surface in the enormous chamber was covered in translucent egg-sacs, and every one of those contained a Nara-Karith. There must have been tens of thousands. As he stood there, staring, he heard a wet tearing just ahead. He peered through the miasma and saw one of the giant insects hatching out of the mucus-filled bag.

'They're hatching,' muttered Dray, awestruck.

The three of them were prodded forward down a tight path between the sleeping aliens. Bile rose in Ayl's mouth as a powerful psychic presence swept over him. It paused momentarily, recognizing his mind, then moved on, probing its sleeping children. The queen was near.

Ayl's revulsion was like a physical force, pushing him back the way he'd come. He had to command himself to keep going, to fight against the fear itself. More of the bugs were escaping their containers as they passed, like dreadful pylocanths emerging from spawn. Each one dropped to the floor, shook itself, then scuttled over to join its brethren guarding the teenagers. Soon they were surrounded by hundreds of the creatures. Eventually, they came to the darkened entrance of another tunnel and the Nara-Karith stopped. The three of them stood there uncertainly, a dark cavern ahead and a horde of predators behind.

'What now?' asked the trade prince. He was clearly hoping not to have to continue. Ayl knew there was no other option. He could sense the queen ahead, her thoughts feeding into all of the aliens behind them. They were surrounded, not by a mass of insects, but by a single mind.

'We keep going,' he replied and walked into the darkness. Behind him he heard the Cantorian mutter something unholy, and then Keller ran to catch up. The three of them walked on together.

The tunnel grew darker, with fewer lights studding the ceiling. The walls were covered in what looked like thick veins, pumping liquids down to whatever was waiting for them at the end. There was a cloying mist reaching ankle height. None of the Nara-Karith followed them in and Ayl didn't see a single one of the monsters as he walked. The tunnel turned in a slow arc, barely noticeable, but after about two hundred paces they could no longer see the entrance. A little further on and the passageway ended in a flat wall. The three of them stopped a short distance away and Keller threw up his hands in frustration.

'A dead-end!' he cried. 'What in—'

Before he could finish Ayl cried out in agony. A sharp flame leapt up into his mind, disappearing almost as suddenly. The Aquanth looked at his friends.

'She is here,' he said simply.

As he spoke a vast black shape loomed out of the mist in front of them. Dozens of incredibly long spikes pierced the fog all around the shape, writhing and twisting in a horrific dance. Legs whipped through the air as the gigantic beast reared up, dwarfing the teenagers before its terrible majesty. Vicious fangs chomped up and down in its appalling mouth. The eyes above were pure evil, malevolent black-holes sucking in all life.

The queen stretched down towards them and roared.

20

The trade prince backed away as the tide of noxious gases from the queen's breath washed over him and the sound subsided. He watched, rooted to the spot, as three humanoid figures were brought up out of the mist.

'By the stars,' muttered Dray, as the thick white gas fell away to reveal their parents.

'Look,' whispered Keller. 'The queen . . . it's got hold of them.'

A leg was wrapped tight around each of the adults' necks. Their eyes were wide open but focused on nothing. Lial and Iccus stood slightly behind the high priestess, all three in thrall to the beast. They looked almost comatose under the alien's mental grip. Lady Moa stepped forward shakily.

'We are the Nara-Karith,' came her strangled voice. Keller saw Ayl begin to move towards his mother, a look of agony on his face. Dray jumped forward to stop the Aquanth, holding him back.

The trade prince grabbed him by the shoulders. 'It's not her,' he hissed. 'It's the queen talking through her! We need to play for time.' A lump formed in his throat as he saw the tears well up in the other boy's eyes, but he turned back to the fiend. 'Why are you here?' he shouted, looking at the woman.

'To feed,' came the chilling answer. 'For countless turns we have wandered. Now we grow hungry again. We will harvest your people. Your three races are barely children compared to us.'

'But we can trade,' said Keller, hoping to find the words that could end a war. 'We are rich. We can give you what you want and you can leave. There's no need for more death.' The high priestess started to make a rapid wheezing sound. He thought for a moment that she was fighting the queen but then he realized what it was. The alien was laughing at him.

'We will take everything,' she replied. 'We will strip your planets bare. We have visited thousands of stars, falling from the sky on unknown numbers of worlds. We leave nothing untouched. When we are finished consuming, we build new nests like this one, and send them out into the cosmos like seeds on the wind. When all of my offspring have hatched we will attack and tear your civilizations apart. You are weak and we are strong. What can you offer that we cannot take?'

'We will fight you,' shouted Dray, stepping forward. Keller saw her looking up at the monster, unflinching. 'With everything we have, we will fight.'

'Then where is your army?' asked the queen, her shuddering laugh coming through the high priestess again. 'Why is it only you standing here? It is too late, you have waited too long. My brood stirs. Soon the Nara-Karith will attack and you will all die.'

Ayl fell to his knees and clasped his hands together.

'Divine universe, please give me strength,' he said softly. He could hear Keller and Dray trying to argue with the devil before them. The Aquanth knew they could never defeat the creature, that soon the Bellori fleet would destroy them all.

Even if we are to die in this darkest of places, I must try to get a message to my mother, he thought. *To let her know I love her.*

He forced his mind to stretch out once more, perhaps for the last time. He saw the chamber in his mind's eye and he was suddenly awash with light. The queen's consciousness reached out along the tunnel, like the trunk of some immense tree, ready to branch out and control the multitude of animals behind them. The strange living tubes along the walls and ceiling pulsed with an even stronger fire. They seemed to focus the alien monarch's thoughts, amplifying them. The very structure they were in was like a great organic machine, powering the alien at the centre of it all.

He turned to his mother, trying to find her thoughts beneath the Nara-Karith influence. The leg wrapped around her neck was like a twisted band of flame leading back into the beast. He followed it, hoping to find a weak point, somewhere to cut the connection, if only for an instant. The limb led him back to the queen's body and the searing heat sent razor-sharp filaments of agony throughout his nervous system. He knew his two friends were close by, unaware of his efforts. But just knowing they were there gave him the strength to press on.

He delved deeper into the alien mentality and it all became clear. What had risen from the mist wasn't the queen. Like a Bellori encased in armour, it was an engineered piece of machinery – alive, like the tunnel itself, but not physically one with the alien. Somewhere within the huge shell was a Nara-Karith, more intelligent than the rest of her species, but still just as mortal. The carapace protected her and focused her psychic ability, allowing her to control all the others.

There is hope! he thought. If he could break the connection, he would end her control of the hive.

He pushed on, through layer upon layer, coming to the single kernel that was the queen's true being. It was joined to the rest by a tiny thread, so thin when seen alongside her amplified majesty.

I have you. He reached in and the thread suddenly flared into a towering inferno. He tried to take hold of it, snap it apart. The heat raged away at his being and images of burning flesh filled his mind. *I will not let you go!* The creature roared in pain and he was engulfed in fire.

Focus, Ayl, came the voice of his mother. *Focus.*

Mother! he cried. The queen was crushing him now. The pressure at the ocean floor was nothing compared to this.

Focus.

He saw the thread again. Slowly, forcing himself forward, he reached out, fighting against the fire-storm buffeting him. It was in his hands and he pulled.

The intense light blinked out in an instant and he opened his eyes, hoping with all his being that it was over.

His mother and the two other adults slumped to the

ground as the legs around their necks went slack. The monster's body seemed to be going into convulsions and a huge cracking sound came from its shelled torso. With a spray of dark green slime, the immense form split in two to reveal a mess of lumpy mucus.

Ayl stood up on shaky legs and took a step forward. Keller and Dray were standing stock still, looking at the huge mess of insect parts. Everything was quiet for a click. Then the queen showed her true form, rising from the slime, identical to her smaller brethren in shape but twice the size. The three friends stepped back as the creature stood and stretched, making a horrendous chittering, hissing sound. The alien seemed to lean back on its long legs, almost touching the fog with its body. Then it sprang forwards, razor-sharp legs spread wide and teeth gleaming as it flew through the air. Straight at Ayl.

'No!' cried out Dray, leaping through the air and barrelling into the giant insect. One of its serrated legs caught the Aquanth in the face. She saw her friend go down, a spray of blue blood arcing away from his head, before finding herself falling in a tangled mass of alien limbs.

The creature screeched with rage as they slammed

into the ground. Its body flexed and twisted, its legs kicking and twitching in manic fury.

'Is that all you've got?' she screamed in its face. 'Is that all you've got?' She bear-hugged its torso, rolling through the fog with it in her grasp. Her ears filled with a frantic scratching sound as it tried to tear at her suit. It slashed and cleaved, sending sparks flying from her armour plate. She squeezed tighter.

'You're mine,' she hissed. Her face was just inches from its gnashing jaws. It suddenly wrapped its legs around her and sank its teeth into her helmet. The metal buckled and she felt the tips of razor-sharp fangs nick her cheeks. Her face plate was pulled away with a terrible rending noise and the alien spat it aside. Now there was nothing between her face and the alien's dagger-filled mouth.

She squeezed as hard as she could and felt the queen's torso bend. Her armour boosted her muscles tenfold as she poured every ounce of strength into the embrace. A great cracking sound pierced her ears, followed by a terrible, agonized screech as the beast kicked her away. She went flying through the air and landed with an impact that drove the breath from her lungs.

She got to her feet and cried out as her left knee buckled. *Twisted*, she thought, *must have fallen on it.*

The Nara-Karith was standing now too, flexing its legs. She could see where she'd fractured the creature's shell, blood oozing out and dripping down. All that effort and she'd only managed to scratch the huge alien.

'Dray!' Keller shouted. Out of the corner of her eye she could see him helping Ayl stand.

'Stay back,' she called to the boys. 'I've got this.'

The insect spread its two long legs wide and screamed.

It's up to me, now, she thought. *There's nothing to lose. I'm wounded, my armour's damaged and I'm unarmed.* She smiled. *This is going to be fun.*

'Come on!' she yelled at the monster. 'I'll show you how a Bellori fights!'

Dray charged at the queen. Adrenaline pumped through her system and the pain in her leg disappeared. One of the alien's legs came stabbing in a blur through the air. She turned and it missed her head, gouging a deep line in her shoulder plate instead. The momentum spun her round and she grabbed the limb. Holding tight to the queen's leg, she jumped up and pulled, kicking with both legs against the beast's shoulder. She strained until, with a sickening wet ripping sound, she wrenched the alien's leg free of its joint and fell to the ground with a thud. The injured queen roared in agony and skittered away.

Dray jumped up to her feet and threw the limb aside, every muscle burning. *I need to finish this*, she thought. The alien leapt at her again, its remaining legs slicing through the air. She ducked and forward-rolled under it, coming up beneath the beast's body.

Take it to her, she thought. *I've got to take the fight to her.* She punched up at the queen's torso, again and again, each strike leaving fissures in the shell. The animal screeched and then pounced on her, squashing Dray with her weight. Four powerful legs pinned her to the ground. The Bellori brought her arms up just in time to keep the monster from sinking its mandibles into her head.

'Bad choice,' she spat at it, staring into its eyes as she held it at bay. Both of them strained against each other. The monster's teeth were only clicks away from digging deep into her, tearing her apart. Her shoulders were on fire, her arms trembling under the queen's bulk, her hands on either side of the alien's horrendous face. With a cry of victory, Dray twisted the beast's head right round with a sudden jerk. Its limbs spasmed then it slumped to one side, sliding off her, dead.

21

Ayl watched Dray sit up. The girl winced and let out a long slow breath. He walked over to her with Keller and the three friends looked at each other.

'You were incredible,' said the trade prince breathlessly. 'Are you OK?'

'I'll survive,' she replied, getting to her feet. 'But not for much longer unless we get a move on!' Her knee buckled and the Aquanth put out an arm to steady her. She leaned on the boy and they smiled at each other. 'How are your parents?'

'Alive,' replied the blue-skinned boy, using his hand to staunch the blue blood flowing from the cut on his face. 'Thanks to you.'

An incredible screeching cacophony echoed down the tunnel towards them. It sounded like every Nara-Karith on the asteroid was awake and angry, chittering and screeching like a horde of demons. Ayl glanced nervously in the direction of the sound. If Dray had killed the queen, shouldn't the other Nara-Karith have stopped fighting?

The huge bulk of General Iccus walked up to the three teenagers. As his battered helmet arched back, revealing a face that could have been carved from rock, Ayl felt Dray squeeze his arm tightly.

'General,' she said. The girl brought her free arm up in a salute. The leader of the Bellori snapped his hand up to his forehead in return.

'Dray,' replied Iccus, a smile softening his features. 'You have proved yourself to be a great warrior. I am proud of you.'

And I of you, Ayl, said the high priestess with her mind, standing by the general's side.

I only did what you taught me, he answered, looking up at his mother.

'I hate to mention it,' said Keller, looking embarrassed at having to interrupt. 'But we've got to get out of here. The Bellori fleet is under orders to open fire in fifteen minutes. They're going to blow up this place so the Nara-Karith can't escape. If they make it to our worlds, there will be no stopping them.'

'So what's the plan, son?' asked King Lial.

'Uh . . . We didn't actually get that—' started Keller. Before he could finish, one of the creatures appeared down the tunnel. It sprinted towards them at a terrific speed, screaming the whole time.

I am stronger than you, thought Ayl, stepping forward. He closed his eyes and focused. He fired his mind at the creature like a missile, an arrow of pure mental force. The insect shot straight up into the air with a yelp and came crashing down. General Iccus stomped towards the writhing form and slammed both of his club like fists down on its head, squashing it flat and killing it.

'I've wanted to do that for a while,' said the big man to himself. He turned to the Aquanth, a puzzled look on his face. 'What did you do, boy?'

'It's a long story, father,' said Dray. She picked up the alien queen's torn-off limb and put it under her arm as a crutch. 'But there's no time. Ayl, can you keep them away from us?'

'I think so,' he replied. He looked at the high priestess hopefully. 'Perhaps, with my mother's help.'

I am with you, his mother thought, nodding.

Ayl then looked at Keller, who was helping his father stand. The trade king looked terrible, drawn and pale, but he could see that his son was determined to keep him going. The two of them locked eyes for a moment and nodded. It was time to go.

The two Aquanths led the way back along the tunnel. They could hear the absolute chaos of what was ahead. In the egg-chamber, hordes of Nara-Karith were running rampant, attacking each other and ripping into the young. Hundreds of the creatures piled on top of one another, eating their brethren alive. Individual combats spawned small-scale battles that moved to and fro across the space.

Ayl jumped as something touched his hand, only to realize it was his mother. She looked into his eyes.

We can do this, Lady Moa thought.

Together, he replied.

Their two minds became one. They created a shield to keep the creatures at bay, picturing a thick wall all around them.

'Come,' Ayl said to the others. Slowly the group walked forward. They edged out into the great space and instantly a host of Nara-Karith turned, noticing them. The bugs screamed in rage and charged, stopping dead at the mental blockade, ramming and beating against it. It was like a hundred sledgehammers pummelling his mind.

With only minutes until the bombardment started, Ayl wondered if being blown up would be a blessed relief from this torture.

* * *

Dray stood close to Ayl, watching him tremble with effort. The insects' charge had come to a sudden halt a few paces away. The creatures were forced back for now, hissing and butting their heads against the invisible wall.

'You can do this,' she whispered to the blue-skinned boy. 'I believe in you.' She led the small group out into the chamber. The aliens screeched in frustration, being pushed further and further back.

By the time they got to the centre of the space they were surrounded by thousands of the creatures. They were piled high on top of each other, trying to crawl over their kin to get at the intruders. Their furious shrieking stabbed at her eardrums.

'We can't hold them back,' Ayl yelled over the noise. He was holding his mother's hand and both Aquanths were covered in a sheen of sweat. 'There's too many!'

'Just get us to the tunnel,' she shouted back. She turned to the others. Keller was helping the trade king along, while her father kept watch behind them. 'Come on,' she called out. 'Double time!'

They broke into an awkward jog, trying to keep together. The creatures were pressing in closer and closer. Razor-sharp legs stabbed at them, only to be withdrawn with a scream of pain. She couldn't see the tunnel beyond the mass of alien bodies, writhing and squirming, desperate to get at them.

It's got to be close, she thought. *It's got to be*.

'Hurry – we've only got two minutes!' Dray shouted to the others.

Suddenly the entrance was in front of them and they were running through the passageway. They sprinted on and on, until they reached the site of the ambush. She grabbed a k-gun which had been discarded earlier and spun round as she heard Ayl cry out.

'They're coming,' he screamed, falling to his knees. Behind them she heard the insects roar in fury. They came crashing forward in a wave of black shell and lethal spikes.

'Look after the others!' she yelled at Keller. She knelt down and took aim, facing the enemy.

'A good battle,' said General Iccus, standing to her right and pointing a heavy, multi-barrelled weapon down the tunnel.

The two Bellori opened fire and the first few Nara-Karith dissolved into a spray of alien blood. She poured blast after blast into the swarm, keeping them at bay. There seemed to be an endless torrent of the monsters.

'Krack!' roared her father. He stopped firing as his

weapon ran out of ammunition and he threw the heavy chunk of metal at the bugs instead.

Dray kept shooting until her gun was empty then she jumped up, swinging the rifle like a club. She charged forward with Iccus, into the mass of insects. She punched and kicked, pummelling them for all she was worth, screaming at them.

Suddenly a powerful blast knocked Dray off her feet. She went flying through the air, then found herself lying down, staring dizzily at a flickering light in the ceiling.

The conference centre, she thought. *How did I get here?*

Everything was quiet, the only sound a faint buzzing. Keller and Ayl were standing over her, shouting something she couldn't hear.

'What?' she said. 'I can't . . . My ears . . .' She stood up shakily. Her father pushed her violently aside and she saw him swing a rifle up and shoot. A Nara-Karith dissolved in a spray of slime.

The trade prince had an arm round Ayl and was helping the other boy along. She staggered after them both, grabbing another gun up off the ground. Flames reared up all around and bugs jumped out, only to be shot down by Iccus. Her hearing was coming back and the crackle of fire was all around.

'What's happening?' she tried to yell, her voice sounding as if it was coming from underwater.

'The fleet,' came Keller's reply, muffled even though he was shouting. 'They've opened fire!'

Keller struggled to keep moving. He could barely hold Ayl up with his left arm and the bolt-rifle in his right hand weighed a tonne. His eyes were watering from the smoke that poured from so many fires around them. He tried to blink the stinging pain away and focus on following Dray as she scouted a path through the destruction. The fleet were firing warning shots at the asteroid.

We can make it, he thought. *We can still escape!*

A torrent of flame burst out of a doorway and sent him and the Aquanth flying.

'Ayl,' he cried. There was no sign of his friend, or anyone else, only a raging inferno all around him. A Nara-Karith leapt through the fire only to be crushed by a falling chunk of ceiling.

'Keller!' he heard his father shout. 'Where are you?'

'Don't wait for me!' he yelled back, coughing the acrid smoke out of his lungs. He grabbed a thick sheet of wall panelling from the ground. The trade king's voice had told him where everyone else was – now he just had to get there.

After this, I think a long weekend skiing in the Jikon mountains. Yeah, somewhere nice and cold. He wiped the sweat from his face then held the sheet of metal up in front of himself. Here we go, then.

The trade prince leapt into the fire, sprinting as fast as he could. The backs of his hands were instantly in agony and he screamed in pain. He tripped and went flying forwards, falling on to the metal and skidding forwards. Hands grabbed him and pulled him along, slapping at his clothes.

'You crazy mullock,' laughed Dray, pulling him to his feet.

'I thought I'd lost you,' said the trade king, grabbing his son and hugging him tight.

'I'm OK, Dad,' Keller replied, squeezing him back.

'We don't have time for this,' growled the general.

The hangar bay was still intact when they reached it, the assault shuttle sitting where they'd left it, undamaged. Iccus and Dray ran towards it, checking the area for any Nara-Karith. The rest of the group followed after them. The wall behind suddenly exploded in a gout of flame and a dozen bugs burst out.

'Move,' screamed Dray, firing at the aliens. They ran

as fast as they could. All but one of the monsters fell. The last one was already missing two legs and lurched forward, stretching out the sharp point of one leg. Keller turned back to pull his father out of the alien's reach, but the rage-fuelled creature moved quicker. Lashing out wildly, the creature stabbed its dagger-like leg into Lial's back. The trade king collapsed with a howl of pain.

'Father!' screamed Keller, as Lial crawled away from the alien. As Dray blew the maimed beast apart the trade prince crumpled to his knees by the king's side.

'Can you walk?' the boy asked desperately. The older man was in a pool of blood, trying to stand.

'I'm fine,' he grunted in reply. 'You go ahead.'

'I'm not leaving you,' Keller said, lifting him up to his feet. Draping his father's arm around his shoulder, Keller slowly dragged King Lial towards the shuttle. Everyone else was inside, but Dray was in the shuttle hatchway, firing at something behind them.

'Move, Keller!' she shouted, letting loose a hail of bullets. The firestorm raged around them, as Keller inched closer to the shuttle. Explosions buffeted the Cantorians, knocking them from side to side.

They made it to the small ship, battered but alive, and Keller sealed the hatch. He carefully manoeuvred his father into a seat, then sat down next to him.

'What are you doing?' shouted Dray. 'You've got to fly this thing.'

'I can't leave my father,' said Keller.

'Leave him with me,' said Ayl, placing a reassuring hand on Keller's shoulder. 'I will look after him.'

'Don't worry about me, son,' said King Lial, struggling to turn a grimace of pain into a grin. 'Just get us off this kracking rock.'

The trade prince rushed forward and jumped into the pilot's seat. Iccus had already ignited the engine.

'By the stars,' Keller muttered, looking at the scanners. Nara-Karith were swarming outside, scratching at the hull. He brought the ship up to hover, then activated the thrusters, sending a huge torrent of blue fusion-fire coursing through the chamber, incinerating the aliens. Gritting his teeth, he used the small ship's only weapon, a plasma cannon, to blast a hole through the hangar bay's roof.

Then Keller pulled back the throttle and the plane shot upwards, into space – away from the burning asteroid, away from the raging Nara-Karith.

22

Dray watched through a porthole as the ship flew away from the asteroid. Explosions blossomed across the surface like giant orange flowers. A continuous stream of hyper velocity rounds slammed into the asteroid, sending shockwaves rippling through the huge mass of rock. As she watched, it split slowly in two, then three. More and more fragments drifted apart until all that remained was a collection of boulders. The fleet kept firing, sending in more missiles and energy beams, reducing the rubble even further. The Nara-Karith were no more.

Turning round, Dray saw Ayl and his mother tending to the trade king while the small craft shook under the acceleration. The older man was badly wounded and puddles of blood were forming on the deck plating.

'How's he doing?' she asked.

'He will be fine,' replied Ayl, forcing a smile. His

eyes told her he was lying.

'That's kind of you,' coughed the wounded man. 'But I know I'm finished.'

'Quiet, friend,' said the high priestess, wiping his brow. 'You need to rest, that is all.'

As Ayl attempted to staunch the flow of blood, his mother rooted around inside the ship's medical kit. Lady Moa pulled out a small hypospray, which she put to Lial's neck, injecting its contents into him. His ashen face relaxed instantly and he smiled at the two teenagers.

'Keep an eye on my son for me, eh?' he said. When he grinned, Dray could see how much he looked like Keller.

'Of course,' she replied, feeling a lump form in her throat. 'I'll get him for you.' As she walked towards the forward compartment, she heard the Aquanths muttering prayers. The last rites.

Dray stepped through the hatch and saw her friend and her father sitting side by side at the controls. On the view-screen ahead of them, the asteroid was dissolving in a multi-coloured firework display, tinting their faces with eerie reds, greens and blues. She saw small fighter-class ships diving in, the blue candle flames of their exhausts flaring brightly as they fired particle beams at anything larger than a pebble.

'The king needs you,' she said, putting her hand on the trade prince's shoulder. He looked up and Dray saw his eyes fill with tears.

'Is he . . . ?' Keller began.

'You should go to him,' she replied quietly. He stood quickly but before he could go she quickly embraced him. It felt strange to Dray, as Bellori did not hug each other, but she wanted her friend to know she was with him. As Keller squeezed her back, she felt an uncharacteristic surge of warmth. Then she took his place in the pilot's seat.

'You have accomplished much,' said General Iccus, the bass rumble of his voice breaking through her tiredness. 'You truly are my daughter.' She turned to look at the huge man, a tempest of emotions battering away inside her chest. She looked at the heavy brows and the wide jaw of the man whose acceptance she had always craved. The fading glow of the Nara-Karith hive highlighted the scars that criss-crossed his face, reminders of the endless fighting he had endured, the endless fighting he had dragged his people through.

She knew Keller and Ayl had fought to save their parents as much as their planets. But she had been fighting for her entire life to impress her father.

'What I did,' she said quietly, looking at the

commander-in-chief, 'I did for Bellus, not for you.' Then she turned to the view-screen and steered the ship towards the Bellori fleet.

Keller felt bile rise in his throat and turned away. His father was lying on the floor, as white as a ghost, the Aquanths on either side of him trying to stop the bleeding from a large hole in his abdomen. For an instant, he didn't want to go on. He looked up again to see his father, and knew he had to. He walked in and went down on one knee beside Ayl, the other boy smiling slightly and giving him space.

'I'm here,' he said, putting his hand on the king's face and feeling how cold it was. The man coughed and a speck of crimson fluid appeared on his lip.

'I am so amazed by you,' his father whispered, lifting a trembling hand to squeeze his son's arm. 'You are so much more than I could ever be.'

'Quiet, Father,' Keller said, almost choking on the words. 'You need to rest. We're almost at the fleet. The Bellori doctors will patch you up.'

'I'm finished, son,' replied the dying man. 'My time is over. You are the trade king now.'

'No!' shouted the teenager, tears starting to fall down his cheeks. 'I'm not ready, I still need you! We still need you!' He looked desperately at the Aquanths for help.

'You will be a greater king than I ever was,' said Lial, struggling for breath now. 'I love you, Keller.' The man shuddered once, took a slow, shallow breath, and then breathed no more.

Keller pulled the dead man's head to his chest and rocked back and forth for a moment. 'I love you too,' he whispered, and then laid his father down. He felt numb, unsure what to do, the whole universe suddenly unreal, spinning around him. Then Ayl put his arm round the new king's shoulder and the tears started to fall again. The two boys cried together as the high priestess ran her hand over the dead king's face, closing his eyes.

A few cycles later, Ayl was standing on the observation deck of the Bellori flagship, the *Astyanax*, staring out into space. The high priestess had lifted the Shroud and told her people that the danger had passed. Ayl and his mother were scheduled to take a shuttle back to Aquanthis in less than two hours. He couldn't wait.

I can't wait to tell them about everything I've seen, he thought. He could just picture his friend Wan's face when he told him about all the spaceships.

'Now I wish I was the telepathic one,' came Keller's

voice from the side. The Aquanth turned to see the new Trade King of Cantor approaching, with General Dray by his side. The boy was dressed in a finely tailored roark-silk suit, an incredible contrast to the basic heavy armour the girl wore. 'If only to find out what that smile was for.'

'Just contemplating my return home,' replied Ayl, bowing his head in greeting. 'And looking forward to some proper food. Nothing on this ship can even compare to Thusik tubers.'

'Thankfully,' laughed the other boy.

'I suppose there is no accounting for taste. But seriously, how are you?' he asked.

The Cantorian shrugged, looking a little embarrassed. 'It hasn't really sunk in yet,' he answered. 'I can't believe my father is gone. I guess we'll see how things go once I get home and everything settles down.'

'If you need any help, you only have to ask,' said Dray, looking stern. 'I am more than happy to help with negotiations.'

'Thanks,' laughed Keller, slapping her on the back. 'But I've seen how you negotiate, remember? How am I supposed to make money out of anybody after you're finished with them?' The girl grinned and just shrugged her shoulders, quite happy with her newfound reputation. Ayl had heard some of the other Bellori speak about her fighting prowess with awe.

'But what about the asteroid, Ayl?' the warrior asked him. 'Your scriptures said it was holy, didn't they? I'm sorry that didn't work out for you.'

'It was foretold that the Heavenly Messenger would bring unity to our worlds,' he replied. 'Who are we to say that it hasn't?'

Epilogue

The sleek, black ship dropped silently towards the rock's surface. Dust clouds billowed up around it as the manoeuvring jets fired. The particles sparkled in the weak starlight before falling slowly back to the ground. Landing gears slid out of housings under the craft, and it touched down, twenty solarpaces from where its journey had begun.

A hatch opened on the top of the small vessel and a robotic arm snaked out. At its end was a small sensor array which it turned on the surrounding landscape, scanning the area. The scenery was grey and lifeless. Craters pockmarked the rock's surface but there was nothing else. Not a single footprint or sign of intelligence. The lack of atmosphere stopped any form of known life from taking hold of the rock.

I know they're here, the man controlling the robot thought. *They must be.*

Another, larger hatch opened on the ship. Bright,

white light shone out and showed a gigantic figure. For a moment, he paused. Stepping out on to the rock's surface, he walked away from the craft and moved purposely forward without turning or looking to either side.

He had no idea how far he'd gone when the first flicker of movement appeared in the corner of his eye. Something was circling him. Something big.

He waited.

Twenty paces ahead, a huge, dark insect slowly emerged from behind a boulder. It hissed at the man and snapped its mouth. Two more appeared behind it and the Nara-Karith moved towards him. More and more of the creatures emerged from the ground until dozens of them surrounded him. The first one was close enough to touch now.

'I'm a friend,' said Sudor.